CHARLIE'S MOLASSES

BASED ON A STORY BY MARK RISHER

DONNA M. CARBONE

SEAQUILL PRESS,LLC.

For information contact:
Write For You, LLC
Palm Beach Gardens, Florida 33410
www.writeforyoullc.com
Email: write4you@comcast.net

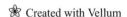 Created with Vellum

"Damn, girl! You can write!"
~ Burt Reynolds ~

ACKNOWLEDGMENTS

A number of very special people contributed to this book by providing us with insights into their family histories and sharing personal stories about what it was like to be "new" to our great country.

We want to express our sincere thanks to Joan D'Hurieux for trusting us with tales of her ancestors, in particular stories about the Maroons living in Jamaica. Her insights on life in the Caribbean added authenticity to our storylines, which would not otherwise have been possible.

We also want to thank Ruth Pador, who helped to clarify some common misunderstandings about race relations between certain Latin American ethnicities. Her experiences as a Cuban American were invaluable in our quest to provide factual information in this book.

Additionally, we want to thank our families and friends for serving as beta readers and editors throughout the writing process. There are many people who deserve recognition for their tireless dedication in reading and re-reading and re-reading this story. They include Mike Carbone, Terry Risher, Michael D. Carbone, Dane Risher, Judie Wilcox and all the wonderful academics and journalists who wrote stories and research papers on the sugar industry in Florida.

Writing this book was an education on many levels. We hope you will be better informed as well as entertained by what you will read on the following pages.

"The best fiction is always based on fact."
Donna M. Carbone

PREFACE

*M*other Nature is a voracious eater. In the Everglades, the immobile... mansions and machinery... are soon devoured by the ever-advancing green overgrowth that is to the earth what skin is to the human race.

Forty-four miles from the luxury of Palm Beach is the deserted town of Bryant. Only two rotted and rusting buildings remain to tell the story of who lived and worked on the land and what became of a once thriving sugar dynasty.

If any ghosts linger there, they are the ancestors of Frederick Edward (F.E.) Bryant, for whom the town is named. Bryant emigrated from England to New Mexico in 1894 to study agriculture. Along with his brother, Harold, he owned a dairy farm in Colorado. During a visit to Florida in 1908, F.E. saw the potential for developing a farming community in the Everglades.

The idea remained but a dream until World War I caused a shortage of sugar. With the blessings of the U.S. Department of Agriculture, Bryant and his partner, G.T. Anderson, started Florida Sugar and Food Products Company. Together, they built the first sugar mill in the Glades in 1921.

Needing capital, Bryant and Anderson decided to merge their busi-

1

ness with Southern Sugar, but the venture began failing 10 years later. In stepped philanthropist Charles Steward Mott, co-founder of General Motors, who bought the bankrupt Southern Sugar, renaming it the United States Sugar Corporation. He built the Bryant Sugar House, the largest and most advanced sugar processing mill in the world at the time. The town of Bryant, where most of the workers lived, sprung up around the mill.

As the country and the economy changed, the demand for raw sugar dwindled. By the 1990s, less laborers were needed as more mechanical harvesters were used. The displaced workers filed a class action suit, which cost the company dearly. In 2007, U.S. Sugar closed the Bryant mill and laid off the remaining workers.

Today, Bryant, which is located on State Road 700 near Lake Okeechobee and the City of Pahokee, has a post office and a zip code. No mail is ever delivered since ghosts have other ways to communicate with the living. While all the streets and signs remain, they are mostly hidden beneath vegetation as Mother Nature reclaims what was once hers and hers alone.

EPIGRAPH

"The dead could only speak through the mouths of those left behind,
and through the signs they left scattered behind them."
~ Robert Galbraith ~

The Vodou priestess told her people of the first of their kind to be fed
to the alligators. The young man had heard the threats that if he did not
do as his master told him, such would be his fate, but he did not
believe.

One evening, while walking through the village, he was grabbed
from behind, a sack thrown over his head. He had no idea where he
was being taken until the sack was removed.

The first thing he saw were the eyes... more eyes than he could
count... glowing in the dark. Then, he saw the teeth.

Even as his clothes were stripped away... even as the molasses was
poured over his naked body, he still did not believe he was about to be
eaten. It was not until the first set of jaws clamped on his face that he
accepted his fate.

The young man was still alive as the alligator began his death roll, spinning and convulsing wildly while tearing off chunks of flesh. No one heard him screaming below the water's surface. No one saw the pupils of his eyes grow large with fear. No one saw the agony on his face as he passed from life to death. No one cared.

PROLOGUE

OKEECHOBEE COUNTY, FLORIDA EDITION   APRIL 2, 2018

THE DAILY NARRATIVE

CARNAGE IN THE CANES

Partial human skeletons found in alligator pit at abandoned sugar mill

 Researchers with the South Florida Ecosystem Restoration Task Force, a division of the Environmental Protection Agency, came upon a gruesome sight while doing a routine check of the Lake Okeechobee watershed. On the grounds of the once thriving Bryant Sugar Mill was an alligator pen hidden by dense overgrowth.

In and around it were dozens of gators, alive and dead. Under the murky waters of the 12 foot deep pond were bits and pieces of human skeletons. Very little information has been released by the EPA. What is known is that a researcher taking photographs of the area captured the image of a human femur caught on a downed tree limb. The FBI was summoned.

A trapper captured the gators and transported them to an alligator farm in Louisiana. The pond, which appeared to be manmade, was then drained, revealing the remains of what could be as many as 50 humans.

Experts surmise that the alligators were caught and brought to the area. The pen was enclosed with a barbed-wire fence, preventing the gators from escaping. The pond was lined with concrete. To survive, the reptiles had to be fed by human hands and, it appears that term might be literal. Along with whatever else they were given to eat, people appear to have been their main diet.

The human remains are being examined by a forensic anthropologist to determine gender, age and time/manner of death. The dead alligators will be examined by a veterinary pathologist.

CHAPTER 1

*W*histling in the wind.

Helen Grant knew the phrase well. She had used it on occasion in her novels. It meant trying to change something that cannot be changed.

Whistling in the wind.

The phrase kept running through Helen's mind as she walked from room to room of her Beacon Hill condo, deciding what to pack and what to throw away. Memories... there were so many memories she wanted to toss into the trash the way her soon-to-be ex-husband had tossed their life together away. She had tried hard to ignore the warning signs. For five years, she had buried her head deep in the sands of denial... so deep that the weight of Roger's lies and transgressions had almost smothered her. Not anymore.

As of this morning, Helen had stopped whistling in the wind.

Although heated, the underground garage where Helen kept her car was cold in the early morning hour. The temperature outside was chilly but held the prospect of a warmer afternoon. The weather forecaster had reported that spring was in the air and, to prove his words were true, he had shown photographs of daffodils poking their yellow heads out of the moist earth. "Spring," he had said, "is a time of rebirth." Helen took his words literally. Today she would be reborn.

A series of shivers raced up Helen's spine and exited at the back of her neck, but they had nothing to do with the weather. She was about to set out on an adventure, and the thought of doing it alone was frightening. Her heart began pounding in her chest as an anxiety attack threatened. Had anyone been standing nearby, they would have heard her mumbling her personal mantra, "I can do this! I can do this!"

Helen rubbed her hands together to distract herself from the nauseating feeling in her stomach. With a harder than necessary slam, she closed the trunk of her car. There was finality in the sound. "I can do this!"

Under the trunk lid were three suitcases packed with business and casual wear made from light fabrics in light colors. On the back seat were four boxes which held her computer, reference books, writing materials and some personal effects that gave meaning to her life. Nothing that connected her to her marriage was among the items. There was a box on the front seat on which she had written "TRASH." She had special plans for that box.

Momentarily, Helen thought of what was left in her apartment... the furniture covered with white drop cloths, the photographs, the china and crystal that had been wedding gifts... all of it a part of her past. She would not look back. The future lay ahead by way of the I-95 south.

At the first rest area after crossing the Sunshine State line, Helen planned to throw the TRASH box in the garbage. In it were three heavy coats, a few hats and several pairs of gloves. Never again would she wear anything warmer than a sweater. Winter and Roger be damned!

The sound and feel of the macadam under the tires changed as Helen drove farther and farther away, leaving the badly in need of repair roadways of the northeast behind. She tuned her radio to the Oldies station and took it as a good omen when the first song she heard was *Good Day Sunshine*, the 1966 hit song by The Beatles. The song had been something of a national anthem for her mom, who had sung it every morning up until her death from breast cancer when Helen was four years old.

Of course, Helen didn't really remember her mother, but her father had kept a photo of her on the mantle in the living room. He included her in all his stories. Irene Grant was always the heroine and remained so in Helen's eyes to this day. That mantle photo was one of the few Helen had packed into the boxes on the back seat.

Spring was in the air, and Helen sang along, believing that the lyrics were a sign from her mother that she had made the right decision.

Good day Sunshine
I need to laugh and when the sun is out
I've got something to laugh about
I feel good in a special way
I'm in love and it's a special day

"Yes," Helen said aloud, "It is a special day. I may not be in love, but I will laugh again, and when I do, my laugh will be loud and strong."

After a moment, Helen whispered, "I miss you, Mom and Dad," as she let the tears run freely down her cheeks.

CHAPTER 2

*A*s a child, Helen Grant would best be described as a tomboy. She was pretty... very pretty, with long, naturally curly, shoulder-length blonde hair that framed her face to perfection. Even while a toddler, she was her father's son in every way. She knew the difference between a Phillips head and a flat screwdriver by the time she was three. She preferred bait fishing to tea parties and fishing waders to party dresses.

Helen's steel blue eyes, inherited from her father Nicholas, were piercing and seemed to look deep into the soul of all she met. Shy by nature, her eyes allowed her to feign interest in the most boring people, a benefit in her career as the author of a well-loved series of novels featuring five globe-trotting young adults. No matter where she went or whom she met, everyone had the "perfect" story idea to pitch to her.

As she grew into a beautiful, independent, determined woman, Helen learned how to use all her attributes to her advantage, and at no time did she need them more than at that moment.

She adored her father and credited him with her success as a writer. It was the stories he had told her every night before bedtime that were the basis for her books. As far as his daughter was concerned, Nicholas

Grant was a God. He was invincible. He was infallible. And, now he was dead. Life would never be the same.

∼

Born in 1948, Nicholas Grant grew up privileged but not spoiled. His maternal grandfather, Victor Waldor, was a well-known oenophile, who had developed a genetically modified Muscadine grape with superior flavor. The wine produced with these grapes was sweet without being cloying. Not only was the fermented juice of the grapes delicious to drink, the grapes were delectable straight from the vine, with flesh that was softer and sweeter than traditional varieties.

The secret to Victor Waldor's success was the insertion of DNA from ancient Roman grape seeds. This produced a grape that was virtually drought, heat and cold resistant, making it immune to climate changes.

The Waldor family owned a prosperous winery in north Florida where all the research and development were done. It was there that Mother Nature gave her seal of approval. On a February night in 1967, a rare hard freeze occurred, wiping out 75% of Florida's grape harvest. Victor Waldor's crop was unscathed, earning him a place in the history books.

As a boy, Nicholas learned to cultivate and care for the grapes that grew in a small patch his "Opa" had created for him.

"Making great wines is a science, Nikki," Opa Waldor would tell him. "You must start from the ground up, literally, if you are to be a great botanist and follow in my footsteps."

In his early teens, Nicholas already knew all there was to know about making wine. From mid-summer to early fall, he could be seen working beside the farmhands, gently clipping clusters of grapes with a secateur and placing them in the small baskets that were spread out between the rows. He knew the ripeness of the grapes merely by looking at them. By the time he graduated from high school, he could speak the language of the "grape" with even the most seasoned growers and scientists. His Opa had trained him well.

Even though Nicholas enjoyed working beside his grandfather, he had no intention of making the winery his life's work. He had dreams of becoming a writer and, when not in school or working at the winery, he could be found with his nose buried in books by Ernest Hemingway, F. Scott Fitzgerald and Joseph Conrad. Hemingway was his favorite, and he longed to sail the seas much as his idol had. Recognizing that his grandson's interests lay elsewhere, Victor sold the vineyard upon celebrating his 80th birthday. He repaid Nicholas' devotion by leaving him a sizable inheritance that gave him the means to pursue his dreams.

As an adult, Nicholas was tall with an athletic physique. He had blue eyes the color of the ocean and wavy brown hair flecked with gold from the many hours he spent in the sun. He had an easy-going smile, which made him an instant favorite with everyone he met.

Not one to indulge in decadent behavior, Nicholas had only three vices — Cohiba cigars, a glass of Hennessey Cognac after a big meal, both in imitation of Hemingway, and sailing. He christened his first boat Pilar, in honor of Hemingway's wife. It was his home away from home until it was destroyed in a hurricane.

Having reached the age of legal autonomy, a reserved but fiercely independent Nicholas had a burning desire to write the next great American novel. Financially comfortable, he bought a 47-foot schooner with the intent to live on it and sail the intracoastal waterways while putting his thoughts on paper. He did not christen this boat, fearing it would be bad luck.

When asked if the boat had a name, he would jokingly say, "Yes. It is named after my first novel. I haven't written it yet."

As driving as was his desire to write, Nicholas lacked the imagination to create a story from nothing. He needed a muse, and he met one in an odd little town called Pahokee, where he docked for repairs to the boat.

And that is where this story begins.

CHAPTER 3

*M*uch as he did not want to name his boat, Nicholas succumbed to pressure from friends and family and christened his soon-to-be home away from home shortly before his departure. He knew that tradition required boats to be named to ward off bad luck. He also knew that thousands of years ago, sailors had named their vessels after gods, goddesses and saints in that hope that good fortune would follow in their wake.

As a man of science, worshipping unseen idols did not appeal Nicholas' nature. Still, he did not want to tempt fate. He was aware that the wrong name was believed to be the reason for sailors becoming lost at sea, the ultimate bad luck.

Since he had no intention of sailing too far from shore, Nicholas was less concerned about a chance visit to Davy Jones' Locker than he was about choosing a name that could impact his future as a successful writer. In the end, his choice was more than appropriate.

～

Typewriter began taking on water as she approached the headwaters of Lake Okeechobee. Having set sail from the City of Stuart, situated on the Atlantic Ocean, without a problem, Nicholas was stumped for a reason. The sloop had traveled the St. Lucie Canal through miles of untouched Florida Everglades and thousands of acres of Old Florida scrub and ranch land without so much as a ripple to disturb the smooth waters under its hull.

Nearly blinded by the bright sun overhead, Nicholas searched the cabin for the *How to Sail* manual he had picked up at a bait shop before casting off two days earlier. Unable to find a hole or lose fitting, he shut down the engine and decided to let the current take the boat toward land. He had no idea where he was or what he would find when he got there... wherever *there* was.

The closer Typewriter drifted toward the shore, the more visible the many vintage signs and billboards that held court against a vivid blue sky became. Their chipped, weathered and worn condition gave testimony to how long the town of Pahokee had held its revered place on the Big O, as Lake Okeechobee was known. The only reason Nicholas knew he was in Pahokee was because the billboard advertising the Good Sam Campground offered a "Welcome to Pahokee" greeting.

As the current became stronger, Nicholas realized Typewriter was headed toward a raised low-lying drawbridge that arched over the waterway. The boat's mast height above the waterline was 19.1 meters. The sign on the bridge warned Nicholas that clearance was 19 meters. With no way to stop the boat from drifting toward the bridge, he began to panic.

Typewriter jolted to a sudden stop as the mast lodged against one of the wooden pylons directly under the raised bridge's deck. The sloop could not continue through and the bridge could not come down. Traffic above was at a standstill.

Nicholas could hear the sound of angry motorists blowing their horns. He tried unsuccessfully to restart the engine. From seemingly nowhere, he heard two voices shouting instructions to him. The bridge master, his scabbed hands gripping the bridge rails, leaned down to get Nicholas' attention. His angry words carried on the wind. "Move the boat! Move the boat!"

Another voice, this one calmer and seeming to be close by, called out to him, "Put up the sail."

Standing on the canal bank under the bridge was a young, school-aged boy. He was barefoot and had his blue jeans rolled to his knees. The fishing pole in his hand was motionless except for the line, which danced in the waves as the waters slapped against the pier.

"Put up the sail," he motioned toward the mast with his free hand.

With only moments to spare before the bridge master lowered the span and crushed the Typewriter, Nicholas sprang into action. He hauled up the sail and the wind blowing under the bridge immediately took control. Typewriter was thrust forward and headed for shore.

Nicholas, relieved and exhausted, turned back to the boy, intending to thank him for his help. Just then, something sharp dug into his neck and Nicholas saw the look of panic on the boy's face. Blood covered Nicholas' hand as he attempted to remove the fishhook caught in the folds of his skin.

"I'm sorry! I'm sorry!" the boy cried, waving his arms frantically while still holding onto the pole. "I was trying to reel you to shore. I'm sorry."

Nicholas was pulled to the edge of the boat and forced to jump in the water as the boy continued to tug unknowingly on the line. The pain was excruciating.

Treading water to stay afloat, Nicholas heard more voices calling to him. A beautiful woman took the rod from the boy's hand and reached into the water to help Nicholas ashore. Her name, Nicholas learned, was Rebecca Bryant.

CHAPTER 4

*R*ebecca Bryant came from money. Her father, Otto Bryant, was unaffectionately called Big Sugar by the residents of Pahokee, the quirky little town he controlled with a mix of money and manipulation. Otto was descended from the Maroons... the African slaves captured by the Spanish and brought to Jamaica to work the plantations. He had been weaned by his father on stories of the Maroon uprising of 1740, stories that told of how the Maroons were willing to give their lives to secure a free future for themselves and their descendants. In business, Otto came to believe any battle was worth the price as long as he won.

Years of interracial breeding had given the Bryant family "a permanent Florida tan." Their skin was a light caramel-color much different from their ancestors. Rebecca was so light, she appeared white. In fact, when standing between the majority of Pahokee's residents, she looked like the cream in the middle of an Oreo cookie. Her eyes were nearly transparent with a hint of amber; her features were delicate, more in keeping with an Asian heritage than her Akan ancestry.

Looking Caucasian in a racially prejudiced world was an advantage for her. Rarely did she correct anyone who assumed she was an exotic blend of Japanese or Vietnamese and French or English. She spared

Nicholas Grant that detail as well when they fell in love and planned to marry. Little did Rebecca realize that lies of omission were even more costly than lies of deception.

~

Unable to loosen the lure from Nicholas' neck, Rebecca offered to drive him to the office of Doctor Richard Dozier, the resident physician. Doctor Dozier was known to everyone as Doc Dick Do. The humorous sobriquet came about when Doc Do's now 60-year-old son entered kindergarten and learned how to play the paper and pencil game with a similar sounding name. He would repeat the three words over and over again, all the while laughing hysterically. The name stuck and became a term of endearment for residents.

Doc Do had an office in the town square just a few minutes' drive from the bridge, where Rebecca's car had been parked on the shoulder. Though in pain, Nicholas studied the surrounding landscape as Rebecca drove. He was surprised to see so many offices and houses built on rises above ground level.

Rebecca explained that the reason was the mineral rich dark soil in which sugar cane, citrus fruits and corn were grown. During rainy season, flooding often occurred, leaving a thick muck everywhere and making the streets impassable. "The Muck" was what the residents affectionately called their town.

At Doc Dozier's office, Rebecca and Nicholas were met by a somewhat aloof receptionist, who told them that the doctor was with a patient and it would be a while before he could see them. Sadie Mae Chosen was in her mid-twenties. She was African American and made no attempt to hide her dislike for Rebecca.

The longer Nicholas and Rebecca were kept waiting, the more impatient Rebecca became. "What is taking Doc so long?"

"Some guy working at the campgrounds tripped and put his leg through a plate glass window," Sadie Mae told them. "It's a deep cut. Doc has a lot of stitching to do."

"Who? Is it anybody I know?" Rebecca's nosiness about every-thing that happened in town was showing.

"I don't think so. He just moved here. His name is Sam Weatherby."

At the mention of Weatherby's name, Rebecca turned red and rushed outside. Nicholas, surprised by her behavior, followed, only to find her pacing the parking lot, a cigarette clenched between her teeth.

"I hate this town and everyone in it."

"Do you have a problem with Mr. Weatherby?"

"No. I don't even know him. It's just the way Sadie was willing to give out information that should remain private. Everybody knows everything about everyone."

"Okay. Let's change the subject. Tell me about your son."

"What son? You mean Charlie?"

"If he is the boy with the fishing pole."

"Charlie is not my son. He's just... a kid. He has a learning disabil-ity. He never meant to hurt you. He gets embarrassed easily. That's why he ran away."

Just then, Sadie Mae stuck her head out the office door and told Nicholas the doctor was ready to see him.

"You don't have to wait for me, Rebecca. I can find my way back to the boat."

"I don't mind waiting. I'll just stay out here until Doc is finished patching you up."

Once Nicholas was out of sight, Rebecca got into her car and started the engine. She sat low in the driver's seat and waited. When Sam Weatherby got into his car and drove away, she followed at a safe distance.

CHAPTER 5

*a*t 82, Doc Dozier was a surprisingly spry man with a full head of white hair and, even more surprisingly, thick dark eyebrows. The eyebrows gave him a Groucho Marx appearance and the thick black glasses perched on his nose added to the illusion. With steady hands, he cleaned the wound before making a small incision to loosen the lure and carefully removing it. Six stitches later, gauze was taped in place and Nicholas was free to leave.

"Thank you so much, Dr. Dozier. I do not know what I would have done if Rebecca had not come to my rescue and brought me here."

"Welcome to Pahokee. We are not a bad bunch despite whatever stories you might have heard."

"Stories? I…"

"Never mind. Keep those stitches dry for a few days. They will self-dissolve. Sadie Mae will give you a sample antibiotics packet. Be sure to take them. Call me if you have any problems."

Back in the waiting room, Nicholas paid the bill and thanked Sadie

Mae for her courtesy. From the doorway to the office, he searched the parking lot for Rebecca.

"Sadie Mae, do you know where Rebecca went?"

"I don't. She never came back inside. I can get you a ride to wherever you're going."

"I need a good mechanic who can fix my boat. Know anyone?"

"As a matter of fact, I do."

Rebecca followed Sam Weatherby to a boarding house on the outskirts of town. Watching him as he attempted to get out of his car, it was easy to see that he was in pain. Rebecca could not have cared less. As far as she was concerned, there would never be enough pain to punish him. But... punish him for what? Even she was not sure where the blame for the misery in her life lay.

Making a change for the better would require Rebecca to accept responsibility for her own misdeeds and, since she refused any blame for her past actions, the reason for her hatred of Sam Weatherby would remain buried in layer upon layer of denial.

"What are you doing here, Sam?"

"You startled me, Rebecca. You are the last person I expected to see in this part of town."

"Answer me. What are you doing here?

"Came to see my mom."

"That should not take more than an hour. Just enough time for her to go to the bank and get you money. There is no need to rent a room or get a job."

"I thought I would stay awhile. See my son. See if he is being cared for properly. Get to know him a little bit."

"I am warning you, Sam. Stay away from me and my family."

"Or, what?"

"You already know what I am capable of doing. Leave!"

Back in her car, Rebecca's calm demeanor shattered. She began to cry, more out of fear than anger. Her carefully orchestrated life was being threatened by the one man who could destroy her future. If Nicholas were to find out…

Bryant Sugar was in danger as well. If her father's business associates were to learn what she had done, it would lead to them knowing all the carefully kept secrets of the Bryant family. Those secrets could never be revealed.

CHAPTER 6

"Uncle Roo? Uncle Noth? Are you here?"

A solid 350-pound sumo wrestler type stepped out from behind a high-crop tractor. The man was so large, the tractor, a massive piece of machinery, looked like a Tonka Toy. Behind him was another man whose familial relationship was never in doubt. The men were clones of each other, both built to do damage should anyone be foolish enough to fight them. The only way Nicholas could tell them apart was by their clothing.

"Mr. Grant. These are my uncles, Roosevelt and Noth Chosen. People refer to them as 'The Chosen Ones.' The big guy in the denim coveralls is Roosevelt. You will hear people call him *Sugar Wrench* because when something breaks down in the sugar cane fields, he is the man they call. Most times, all it takes is a twist of his wrench to get things working again."

Sugar Wrench Chosen extended a hand twice the size of a catcher's mitt. It swallowed Nicholas' hand the way the whale swallowed Jonah in the Bible.

"Nice to meet you, sir. This here is my brother Noth."

Noth Chosen, dressed in grease-stained chinos and a black tee shirt, stuck out an identical catcher's mitt and shook hands. "What can we do for you, Mr. Grant?

"The engine cut out on my boat as I was coming through the channel. I need someone to get it started again."

"You have come to the right place," Roosevelt said, patting Noth on the back. My brother is to boats what I am to tractors. Let us get cleaned up. We will ride out to the marina with you and arrange for a tow."

~

While Sugar Wrench and Noth handled arrangements for the towing and storage of Nicholas' boat, Sadie did her best to become better acquainted with him.

"You're a writer, Mr. Grant? We got lots of stories here in The Muck that deserve telling. Maybe you could stay awhile after your boat is repaired."

Before Nicholas could answer, the brothers returned. Noth was holding an itemized list of what was needed to repair Typewriter.

"Mr. Grant, I am going to have to order some parts for the engine. Won't take but a few days to get here and another five or six days to do the work. If you give me two weeks and $1,200, I will have you back on the water worry free."

Another handshake secured the deal and as Nicholas turned to leave, he said to Sadie Mae, "Seems like I will have time to hear those stories you mentioned. I will be staying on the boat, so you come find me when you have time to talk."

~

The day had been long and exhausting for Nicholas. As the sun set, he eased himself into a comfortable chair on Typewriter's deck, a glass of wine in hand. His eyes were just about closed when he heard angry footsteps coming along the dock.

"Why didn't you wait for me to get a professional to repair your boat. Those Chosen brothers don't know their asses from their elbows." Rebecca stood with her hands on her hips, staring up at Nicholas.

"Excuse me? I haven't seen or heard from you since you left Doc Dozier's office without so much as a "fare thee well" this afternoon."

"I told Sadie Mae to tell you I'd be in touch."

"Well, she did not do that, and it does not matter. I am pretty sure both Roosevelt and Noth know a lot about asses and elbows... and boat engines, too. I'm not worried."

"I wanted to help."

"You can help me to finish this bottle of wine. Interested?"

Nicholas extended a hand to help Rebecca onto the boat.

"I hear you and Sadie Mae are going to be writing stories together."

"Wow! Talk travels with the speed of gale force winds in this town. Where did you hear that?"

"Evening services. She was bragging to her friends that you were going to help her become a published author."

"Not quite, but who knows. The future is, as yet, unwritten."

"I was hoping we could write a book together."

"You... and me?"

"Yes. Why? You think Sadie Mae can write and I can't?"

"Nothing like that. It is just I've never been so popular before. In less than a day, I have two beautiful women wanting to co-write a book with me. What kind of story do you want to write?"

"A love story. What do you want to write about?"

"Charlie."

"What? Why are you obsessed with Charlie? He's nobody."

"I would not be so interested in him if not for the fact that you do not want me to know anything about him. Why is that?"

"It isn't *that* at all. Charlie is... different. He is mentally challenged, but it's more than that. He can do things I have never seen anyone else ever do."

"Like what?"

"He remembers everything you say and can repeat it back to you verbatim months later. He can draw and paint beautiful pictures, but he cannot write his name. Sit him at a piano or hand him a guitar, and he can play even though he has never had a lesson. And he can say the alphabet backwards but not forwards. He's weird."

"He is a savant."

"A what?"

"A savant. That is someone, perhaps with significant mental disabilities, who demonstrates abilities far in excess of an average person. He can play musical instruments by ear. He just needs to hear a song played once and he knows all the notes and chords. He can draw and paint, but I will bet he only draws things he has already seen. He cannot paint from his own imagination, much like I need a muse to write my books. Unlike me, who has already forgotten what I ate for dinner an hour ago, Charlie has absolute recall when it comes to memory. Those are all common traits for someone with savant syndrome."

"He's still weird."

"Let's talk about something else. Tell me about yourself. Tell me who Rebecca Bryant is under the designer clothes, fake fingernails, and $100 haircut."

"Do you really think I am beautiful?"

Two glasses of wine became two bottles of wine which became two people wrapped in an amorous embrace. The moon was high in the sky and hours later, it was replaced by the sun breaking the horizon, and still those two people were wrapped in each other's arms.

The sounds of the marina coming to life awakened Rebecca.

"Oh, shit. We fell asleep. If my daddy finds out I did not come home last night, there will be hell to pay."

"I thought you were an independent woman. You told me you got an engineering degree in college. Engineering is a man's world. Why do you give a damn what your daddy thinks?"

"I don't, but you should. Daddy is not the understanding type when it comes to men and his daughter."

"Nice of you to warn me."

"If you had known in advance, would it have mattered?"

"Not for a second."

"Good. Meet me at Bryant Sugar at three this afternoon. Ask anyone. They can tell you how to get there."

CHAPTER 7

$\mathcal{B}$ryant Sugar was a moderately-sized sugar mill three miles out of town. On the surrounding land not used to grow sugar cane, two and three room houses were nestled closely together. The houses were little more than shacks, made from wood and having only the barest of necessities. Bryant Village, as the townspeople mockingly called the settlement, had been built by Otto Bryant to house the migrant workers who kept his sugar cane business running. He was their lord and master in all ways, though no one would dare to speak those words aloud.

As Nicholas pulled into the unpaved parking lot, he saw Rebecca's Cadillac and took the space next to it. Uncertain where to go, he spent a few minutes studying the landscape. The sugar cane fields stretched far into the distance. He could see men and women hard at work preparing the canes for harvest. Others were transporting the canes that had already been cut to the mill. The place buzzed with activity. There was a good reason why Otto Bryant was referred to as Big Sugar. The mill was thriving.

"Nicholas, over here." Rebecca waved from the doorway of a once new, now rusted metal building that served as the office for Bryant Sugar.

"You're alive. I am assuming your father is none the wiser about your activities last night."

"Hush your mouth, sir. I am a respectable southern girl. I have no idea to what activities you are referring," Rebecca laughed.

Unexpectedly, Nicholas silenced her laughter with a quick kiss. "You may have forgotten, but I remember every detail."

Fingers barely touching, they walked into the office.

～

"Daddy, this is Nicholas Grant, the man I told you about."

"Pleasure to meet you, Mr. Grant. How's the neck?"

"Fine, sir. Thank you for asking. Rebecca was my Florence Nightingale. Don't know what I would have done had she not been there."

"She is a good girl, my daughter. Don't know what I would do without her either. She left a successful career to come home and help her daddy, and I am grateful."

～

Rebecca and her father spent the next two hours giving Nicholas a tour of the mill and the fields. They filled his head with stories of Pahokee and the many *characters* who had lived and still lived in the area. Interestingly, not once during those hours did Otto or Rebecca mention Charlie and, to Nicholas, he was the most interesting person he had yet to meet.

By the time the tour was over, Nicholas was a veritable expert on the community. He knew that Pahokee meant grassy waters in the Creek language. He also knew that in the 1930s, the area was considered to be the winter vegetable capital of the world. During that decade, the town had been alive 24-hours a day with long trains of refrigerated cars rolling in and out for the northern markets. Along with bars and restaurants that never closed, the roll of the dice could be heard at any hour as gambling halls flourished. Nicholas was surprised to learn that his favorite country music star, Mel Tillis, had lived nearby.

"Well, Mr. Grant, what do you think of our little town now," Otto asked as the trio returned to the parking lot.

"I am impressed. Pahokee has quite a history."

"I'm glad you feel that way. Why not join us for dinner tonight? The Mrs. would love to meet you and she has a few more stories I believe you will find interesting."

"Just tell me where and when."

Dinner proved to be both a delicious and enlightening affair.

Sandra Bryant was Rebecca's stepmother but, having come into Rebecca's life when she was a toddler, she was mom in every way. A beautiful, charming and spirited woman, she grabbed Nicholas in a hug so tight he feared Otto might become jealous. He need not have worried.

"Let the man go, Sandra. We don't want to scare him away before he gets to taste the wonderful meal you have made for us."

"Otto, you know damned well I did not cook us a meal, which is why it will be delicious. Eloise is a miracle worker in the kitchen. The only thing I know about cooking is that I do not like doing it."

"Momma, if anyone is going to hug Nicholas like a bear, it is going to be me. I saw him first."

The laughter that followed lightened everyone's mood as the foursome made their way to the dining room. Sandra talked non-stop about her newest extravagance, a desktop computer. "I used to think an electric typewriter was a modern miracle. Computers can do things far beyond what I ever imagined. You should buy one, Nicholas. It will make writing your books so much easier.

Rebecca told me you are a fan of Hemingway. Being a southern girl, I found his writing to be a bit plain, but I did so enjoy the way his characters spoke. I could almost hear their conversations in my head.

Of course, I am no expert on literature, but I do enjoy reading in the evenings. Good stories engender good dreams.

Oh, just listen to me running off at the mouth. I am going to be quiet now and let you do the talking. I want to know everything about you. Where is home? How did you get here? What are your plans for the future? Are you married, divorced, looking? As I said, I want to know it all. Tell me..."

"Sandra, enough! For someone who claims they will now be quiet, you make a lot of noise." Otto smiled adoringly at his wife and she, in turn, pretended to blush her way into silence.

Conversation around the dining table never ceased. There was a feeling of having known each other for a long time rather than just a few hours. Nicholas made an impression on Otto when he talked about his grandfather and how he had worked beside him from the time he was a child. Otto knew of Victor Waldor's work and said that he held his scientific research in high esteem.

The hour grew late. Sandra and Otto excused themselves, explaining that they were early risers. Rebecca and Nicholas remained in the living room talking in hushed tones.

"Daddy and Momma like you. I suspect they are hoping we will have a future together."

"We have just met Rebecca and, while I would not mind a future with you someday, for now I think we should focus on that book you want to write. Tell me what you have in mind."

"It is about two people from very different backgrounds. They both come from financially secure families, but where the boy is socially acceptable, the girl is hiding a secret that she fears will be her undoing."

"It is said that the best authors write about what they know. Do you have a secret that you aren't telling me?"

"Maybe." Rebecca silenced any further questions with a long, lingering kiss. Thankfully, the sofa was well made and did not make a sound as the kiss became something much more intimate.

The next morning, just before the sun broke the horizon, it was Nicholas running for his car.

CHAPTER 8

*W*hile Noth repaired the boat's engine, Nicholas sat on deck and made notes on a pad of all the stories he had heard about Pahokee and its residents. He also began an outline of the love story Rebecca had pitched to him. He wondered if he could combine Rebecca's concept with all that he had learned and write an epic novel that would take the publishing world by storm.

The first step was to list all the people he had met and those whose names he had heard but whom he had yet to get to know. There were the kindly Doctor Dozier and Grover, the whiskey-loving bridge master who had yelled to Nicholas to "Move the boat." Rebecca had described Grover as, "… a grumpy, wrinkled old hunchback who was more bark than bite."

There was, of course, Sadie Mae and her uncles, Roosevelt and Noth Chosen. Nicholas already considered Sugar Wrench and Noth friends, but Sadie Mae was a bit of a mystery. He would need to make time to talk to her about the story she wanted to write and, in the process, he hoped to discover more about her.

Otto had warned Nicholas to beware of Lamont Minor, a belligerent young deputy with a penchant for arresting people for no good reason. He was believed to be sweet on Sadie Mae, who showed no interest in him.

The thought of Otto brought back a memory from dinner at the Bryant house a few nights earlier. Eloise Weatherby, the cook, had struck Nicholas as an interesting person. Rather, it was the way she was treated by Otto, Sandra and Rebecca that was interesting. They seemed to fear her. There were moments when Nicholas had wondered who was the employer and who was the employee.

Somewhere in her mid to late 50s, Eloise was approximately the same age as Sandra, but where Sandra was self-centered and self-indulgent, Eloise had a world-weary look about her. Her eyelids drooped, either because she was overworked and over-tired or because she hated her employers and keeping her eyes lowered prevented them from seeing the depth of her hatred. Nicholas had the feeling it was the latter reason.

The lists of people and places covered a dozen lined sheets of paper. Nicholas would need to include some of the Haitian workers who labored in the sugar cane fields, especially the woman who sang at the top of her lungs all day long as if she hadn't a care in the world. There was something mesmerizing about her voice. She seemed to control the others merely by singing. Nicholas made a note on the pad. *Voodoo priestess?* Now, wouldn't that add a new dimension to the story.

In time, Nicholas would learn much about voodoo, including the fact that the common spelling was incorrect. Vodou, contrary to his belief that the worshipers were possessed by a devil, was about the union between humans and a divine spirit... a spirit that overtook them through the beat of the drums, dancing and singing.

Nicholas smiled as he reviewed his notes, anticipating bringing these people to life on the pages of a book. The only problem was that the key character... the one person who could set this story apart from all others... was missing. Charlie! He had to find Charlie.

Every afternoon after Rebecca finished helping her father at the sugar mill, she and Nicholas would meet and work on their combined love story/Pahokee-based novel. The more they wrote, the more the story resembled an onion... it had layers — lots and lots of layers — that made it interesting on many levels.

Rebecca's knowledge of her childhood home allowed Nicholas to craft settings and scenarios that sounded real because they were real. His imagination and his increased exposure to the residents of Pahokee, provided the means to create three-dimensional characters. He imagined himself winning a Pulitzer Prize for literature and even wrote the speech he would give when accepting his award.

Of course, Rebecca would be at his side during the celebrations that would follow. Their love for each other was growing stronger, and Nicholas could no longer imagine a future without her in it.

Six weeks passed in the blink of an eye and, finally, the preliminary manuscript was ready to send to literary agents and publishers. Anxiously, they wanted for responses, and they got them. Rejection after rejection after rejection.

Rebecca was angry that these so-called experts could not see the uniqueness of their story, but Nicholas understood why the manuscript had been turned down. He knew in his heart that Charlie was the key to their success. Now, all he had to do was find him without Rebecca knowing he was looking for him.

CHAPTER 9

 he death of her father had left a gaping hole in Helen's life. Her husband's betrayal of their marriage vows had added to the pain that already lay heavy on her heart. Other than her writing, Helen had nothing and no one to help fill in the many lonely hours of the day and night; and since writing is a solitary endeavor, her tendency toward reclusiveness was threatening her sanity.

Helen knew she needed to reconnect with her roots and what better way than to visit the magical places her father had told her about during her childhood. These were the places that were the basis for her stories and, right now, she could use a little magic in her life.

Plotting a course using her in-dash navigation system, Helen decided to take the road trip she had dreamed about for years. The first stop on her itinerary was Connecticut, where she spent a day at Mystic Seaport. Mystic, the charming village that had been featured in the movie Mystic Pizza, was only an hour and 45 minutes from her home in Massachusetts. The decision to stroll along the beautiful waterfront had been genius. Helen felt her body relaxing. She was breathing easier than she had in months.

Back in the car, Helen put the pedal to the metal and continued her journey. She decided to by-pass tourist attractions in New York and New Jersey and chose to visit Philadelphia instead. The City of Brotherly Love, famous for its cheese steak sandwiches, was the perfect place to grab a bite to eat. She visited Independence Hall and saw the Liberty Bell, historic sites she had written about but never actually seen. On the road again, she decided to spend the night at the Inn in Montchanin Village, located in Wilmington, Delaware.

Day two took her to Baltimore and, no sooner did she see the road signs for Nick's Fish House, than her mouth began watering for Maryland's famous crab dishes. Since the hour was still early, Helen visited the home of one of her favorite authors, Edgar Allan Poe. She badly wanted to take a sailing tour around Baltimore harbor, but a slight rain had begun, so she decided to come back in the near future and complete her visit. Crab cakes were still on the menu for lunch.

It was but a short drive from Baltimore to Alexandria, Virginia, where Helen had a room waiting for her at The Morrison House Hotel. After walking along the National Mall and ducking into several of the Smithsonian museums, she spent another peaceful night unplagued by the nightmares of the past.

The Airborne and Special Operations Museum in Fayetteville, North Carolina beckoned. The museum offered an awe-inspiring look at the equipment and missions of the U.S. Army's Special Forces division. From there, Helen traveled to South Carolina, which would be her last stop before passing through Georgia and crossing the state line into Florida. Just 25 miles north of Florence was the historic village of Latta, the home of the prestigious Abington Manor.

The Inn consistently won the prestigious Four Star rating from the Forbes Travel Guide, and Helen immediately saw why. The two-story brick structure, once the home of prosperous farmer James H. Manning, was gorgeous. When the sun came up over the horizon, Helen had a difficult time bidding goodbye to the owners, who were originally from Miami. Over drinks in the lounge the evening before, they had talked to Helen about what to expect when she reached her destination.

WELCOME TO FLORIDA
THE SUNSHINE STATE

While Helen was tempted to spend time in St. Augustine, where she would supposedly find the Fountain of Youth, the lure of her final destination was too strong to resist. After a quick stop to use the facilities at the rest area just over the Georgia state line, Helen was back on the I-95 south and heading for the City of Stuart in Martin County. This was where her father had started his journey aboard the Typewriter many years before... a journey which eventually took him to Pahokee and a new life.

Helen would not be traveling by boat, so her perspective of the town her father had painted in words of vivid color was going to be very different, but at that moment, she was filled with anticipation for what lay ahead.

CHAPTER 10

*U*pon reaching the shores of Lake Okeechobee, Helen's reaction was much the same as her father's had been more than 40 years before. Amazement! The lake's water extended far beyond what the eye could see. Helen stopped the car to take in the view. She tried to imagine how her father had felt, alone in a sailboat, on this vast inland sea.

A roadside marker informed her that she was in Port Mayaca. The sign also detailed how the lake was divided between Glades, Okeechobee, Martin, Palm Beach and Hendry counties. All five counties met at one point near the middle of the lake. Only God knew exactly where the middle was located.

Helen had driven east to west from Stuart along State Road 76, also known as Kanner Highway, until she reached Lake O. She was very near to her final stopping place, and excitement was bubbling up inside of her. A directional sign advised Helen to follow the road around the lake for 13.4 miles. At the end, she would find Pahokee... and she did, but not the Pahokee her father had painted for her in his stories.

Helen's first impression after parking on Main Street was that either her father had lied or that the passage of time had not been kind to the town and its residents. Her eyes were drawn to a large stucco structure, once painted a pastel pink and white and now faded to the palest shades of both colors. The building's design was reminiscent of art deco. There was a sign on the marquee announcing that this had once been the Prince Theater.

The building was, obviously, abandoned and had been that way for many years. In another city, the theater would have been a tourist attraction and, most likely would have been used for special events. A sadness settled over Helen, which she tried to shake off as she took in her surroundings.

Rather than having her spirits lifted, Helen was filled with a sense of dread. She was tempted to get back in her car and drive away. But... no. She was on a mission and she would not be deterred.

She began to walk and, eventually, came upon another abandoned structure. Pahokee High School — the original Pahokee High School. The cornerstone on the building was etched with the date 1930. Much like the Prince Theater, the school was shuttered and covered in mold. There was a small sign announcing that the school was listed on the National Register of Historic Places, but it did not seem as though anyone in town felt a special pride in that designation.

Disillusioned, Helen began the trek back to her car. She scanned the street, looking for signs of the town that had existed when Nicholas lived here. If that town had ever been, it was long gone.

In the distance, Helen saw what she assumed was a house. It was a fairly well-maintained structure, unlike the buildings surrounding it. Hanging from an L-bracket on the wall facing the street was a sign that read, "Psychic Readings by Lillian."

"Now, is that not fortuitous," Helen said aloud. "So far, the past has been a disappointment. Maybe, it is time I got a glimpse into the future." Making a fist, she knocked lightly on the door.

A voice from an unseen intercom startled Helen, causing her to jump back. "The door is open, Helen."

~

As a child, Madam Lillian had been fascinated by the spiritual world...

not so much the spiritual world of the soul as the spiritual world of the damned. Her grandfather had filled her head with stories of witchdoctors who could perform the "seeing dance" that foretold the future. In her mind's eye, she saw images of black bodies drenched in sweat, prancing around the campfire flames. She had longed to be like those men… to control the minds of others and make them indebted to her through a mix of fear, confusion, ambition and greed.

Now a somewhat frail older woman, Madam Lillian made a living as a psychic. Much like Rumpelstiltskin, she had the ability to spin her tall tales into gold, and desperate and lonely people were willing to pay plenty for any glimmer of hope she could give them.

CHAPTER 11

*D*ressed in a loose blouse with puffy sleeves and a mid-calf skirt of many colors, Madam Lillian sat at a table covered with a cloth that reached to the floor. Around her waist was a long sash and a leather belt with gold coins dangling from gold clasps. Her long, curly, unkempt hair was covered with a scarf, worn low on the forehead and tied in the back. From her earlobes hung over-sized gold hoops that touched her shoulders. On her wrists were enough bracelets to reach to her elbows, and her fingers glimmered with rings on all 10 of her fingers. Her feet were clad in soft ankle-length boots. If ever a character had stepped from the pages of a book into real life, Madam Lillian was her.

In the center of the table was a glass globe filled with a hazy substance that made seeing through it difficult. A deck of tarot cards lay face down next to a small pile of tea leaves. All the tools of a fortune tellers trade were in evidence, and Helen had no doubt Madam Lillian knew how to use them.

"How do you know my name?"

"I know many things about you, while you know nothing about me. I know much about your father, while, again, you know little about him."

"What could you possibly know about my father?"

"I know that he once loved a woman of color and she loved him more than life itself?"

"What? No. My mother was Caucasian."

"She came later. You look just like him. If I did not know better, I would think you were Nicholas in drag."

"You are a wicked woman." Helen turned to leave, but Lillian reached out a hand to stop her.

"Stay. You have come in search of answers. I have them for you, along with stories you have yet to hear and the truth about many you have already heard. Sit down."

With the front door locked and lights turned low so they would not be disturbed, Madam Lillian prepared to take Helen on a journey that would go back in time four decades.

"I do not need a crystal ball to see into the past and the future. Your future is tied to your father's past but not the past as you know it. I knew your father a long time ago, when he was a young man on a quest. He was searching for himself and hoped to find the person he wanted to be by becoming a famous author."

"My father was a good storyteller, but he had no interest in becoming an author. He was a newspaper reporter."

Lillian reached across the table and lifted one of Helen's hands. She turned it palm side up and traced Helen's lifeline with her finger.

"The story I am about to tell you is long, but you will not grow weary from listening… and listen you must for the answers to all your questions are there for you to discover. Do you agree?'

"Yes."

"Then, I shall begin.

You know that your father arrived in this town when he was a young man in his 20s. His sailboat had engine troubles, and he was forced to stay here while repairs were made. What should have been only a two-week delay became a many months long stay during which he made many friends and fell in love."

"I…"

"No. No questions. You must listen until I am through. Yes?"

"Yes."

"The woman your father fell in love with was very beautiful, but she was not who she professed to be. Her name was Rebecca Bryant. Rebecca's family was very wealthy. Her father, who owned the sugar cane fields on the outskirts of town and the mill which processed that sugar, was a powerful man… an evil man. Everyone knew but everyone was afraid to speak of the atrocities he committed, including his daughter.

Your father, being an outsider, was ignorant to the truth. He thought this man was good and kind. When Nicholas asked for permission to marry this man's daughter, he gave it readily, hoping the marriage would give the family more legitimacy.

Why, you are probably asking yourself, would a successful, wealthy family need legitimacy. Forty years ago, only white men ruled the world markets. Otto Bryant looked like every white man living in Florida. He had a perpetual tan which wasn't a tan at all. Under his skin, he was someone very different. And so was his daughter.

If you know anything about race relations, which you should living in Boston, you know that the Irish and the Italians dislike one another, as do the Japanese and the Koreans, the Dominicans and the Puerto Ricans and the Haitians and the Jamaicans. These ethnicities and many more have a long-standing hatred in their hearts for each other. The majority of Otto Bryant's fieldworkers were Haitians. They were forced to swallow that hatred along with their daily bread because, without Otto, they would starve.

Otto was a brutal taskmaster.

In her early teens, Rebecca began rebelling against her father's dominance. When she turned 16, she ran away. For years, no one knew where she was living. When she returned, she was nearly 20. She did not talk about where she had been or what she had done and, for once, Otto was smart enough not to ask questions. He sent her to college. She got good grades and, when she graduated, she went to work for him, helping to run the mill. That is when she realized the truth in the adage, "Ignorance is bliss."

It was not until many years later that the truth about those missing years was learned, but few people were daring enough to speak them out loud. It was said that Rebecca had hooked up with a small-time criminal who was in and out of jail with the speed of a Jack-in-the-box. She had become pregnant, but not wanting the responsibility of a child, she ran away from him as well. The father tried to raise the boy, but prison cells do not a nursery make. His mother and father stepped in and took charge.

There was a continual stream of men willing to take care of Rebecca but, eventually, the desire for her former life of luxury brought her home. The baby was never mentioned.

The hour is getting late and there is something I would like to show you before the sun goes down. Come with me."

"Where are we going?"

"To the marina."

CHAPTER 12

"This is the marina?" The disbelief in Helen's voice was evident as she pulled into a parking space. The lot was an obstacle course of broken macadam, weeds and potholes.

What had once been a thriving waterfront was now a sad reminder of better days. Rotting decks, piers missing half their length, and majestic boats that had become ghost ships were all that was left.

"This is what remains of the old waterfront. The vacant land to the left is where the water department was located and across the street... that building is the original city hall. Like so many other once beautiful buildings, it is scheduled to be demolished. The mayor and council keep plowing our history under the earth or carting it away to landfills. Pahokee has a beautiful new marina and campground, but this... this is where your father lived when he arrived in town."

"He lived here? Where?"

"Follow me."

At the farthest end of the shoreline was a dilapidated sailboat tied to a huge banyan tree. The host tree was 20 feet away, but over the years, its aerial roots had spread out and formed a grove near the water's edge. The tree canopy provided shelter and anchor for the boat.

"I would not have seen this vessel if you had not shown me. The trees… the water… there is a feeling of tranquility here. If I were a pirate, this would be my hideout."

"Feel free to make it so. This is your father's boat. Nothing has been touched. It is as he left it."

Helen looked for a safe place to board the schooner and, with hesitant steps, she made her way to the upper deck. The boat creaked under her weight; the wood unaccustomed to anything heavier than a sea gull walking its planks.

Once confident she would not fall through to the lower deck, Helen went below and entered the mahogany cabin of her own free will. The bunk, the desk, her father's books and papers… except for the dust and cobwebs, the cabin looked as if Nicholas had stepped out for a few minutes. A tuxedo was lying in a heap in a corner, as though it had been kicked hurriedly away. Overcome with emotion, Helen sat down and cried a torrent of tears. Lillian watched from the doorway.

"Forgive me," Helen's embarrassment showed on her red cheeks. "I am not usually emotional."

"No one is judging you."

"I would like to spend the night here. Will that be all right?"

"Of course. It's your boat."

I will take you back to your house…"

"No need. I know my way. Lock the cabin door. Vagrants have been known to wander this area at night."

Helen had no intention of sleeping. She spent hours going through her father's belongings. When she found the manuscripts for the stories he had told her as a child, she settled down on the bed and began to read. Exhaustion overtook her. Her eyes closed and the doorway between the past and present opened. Willingly, she stepped through.

Like a Hollywood movie playing on a big screen, she saw her father lifting her in his arms and tossing her into the air. She squealed in fear and delight as he caught her and whirled her around. Over and over, father and daughter played this game, their laughter making music that even a nightingale would envy.

The scene suddenly changed. Helen saw herself standing on a dock; a boat was anchored nearby. On the transom was painted a strange word — *Qwerty*.

Helen awoke in a sweat. She removed her sweater and shirt and wrapped herself in a sheet from the bed. The dream had awakened a memory. It was too late and too dark to venture outside, yet Helen was certain that outside was where she needed to go.

CHAPTER 13

Footsteps on the upper deck awakened Helen. The smell of fresh coffee brought her upright in the bed.

"I brought breakfast." Lillian knocked on the cabin door.

"Give me a few minutes to get dressed. I will meet you top side."

The hour was early, with the sun just breaking the horizon. "Paradise!" Those were the first words Helen spoke to Lillian as she took the hot cup of liquid fuel from her hand.

"Thank you. I needed this."

"Did you sleep well?"

"Yes and no. I found my father's manuscripts. The stories were the same except for the additional details he scribbled on the sides of every page. The things he wrote... they were... scary. I had nightmares."

"Small town mysteries. They make for the best fiction."

"This was not fiction. For example, my father described Rebecca in detail. You could be her twin."

"Distant relatives. Facially, we look alike. Who Rebecca was and who I am... that is very different."

Lillian watched as Helen collected her thoughts, preparing for the interrogation that was about to start.

"Tell me about their wedding. Something terrible happened... something that made my father fear for his life."

"The wedding was to be a beautiful affair. Important people were invited. Nicholas wanted to wait until the heat of the summer had passed, but Rebecca was insistent that they marry quickly. Within a month, the date was set and the invitations send out. Eloise, the family cook, planned a wonderful dinner. The house, where the ceremony was to take place, was lavishly decorated.

Rebecca had ordered her gown from a store in Palm Beach. It was a designer original and cost her father a fortune. He didn't care. The idea of his daughter marrying a man like your father added to his sense of self-importance."

"I sense this story is not going to have a fairy tale ending. What happened?"

"Are you familiar with the saying, 'Red sky at night, sailor's delight. Red sky at morning, sailors take warning."

"Yes."

"The morning of the wedding held no portent of terrible things to come. There was not a cloud in the sky. The guests were to begin arriving at two in the afternoon. The ceremony was to be at four, with dinner following.

Just before noon, there was a disturbance in the fields. The workers had not been happy for some time. Otto Bryant could be... was a cruel man."

"What did he do that made him 'cruel?'"

"He controlled their wages and paid them poorly. He owned the shacks they lived in and charged them outrageous rent. He charged them to ride the bus that took them back and forth to town, and he owned the general store where they shopped. His prices were three times what other stores would charge. There was no way the workers could afford even the barest of their needs, so he provided credit and kept them indebted to him until they died in the fields or worse."

"He sounds like a slave owner."

"That is how he saw himself. There had been fights between the field hands and the foremen who carried out their boss' orders. The fights were not serious, but Otto did not tolerant dissent. Those workers who defied him were fired and forced to leave the village quickly without even telling their families that they were going."

"That is odd."

"Not really.

So, the wedding... Nicholas arrived in a tuxedo that Rebecca had rented for him from the same store where she bought her wedding gown. The best man was Lamont Minor. Lamont was a town deputy. He and Nicholas were not really friends, but they liked each other and, since Nicholas did not know a lot of people, Lamont was happy to oblige.

Rebecca did not have a lot of friends, either. She asked her step-mother to be her matron of honor."

"Oh!"

"Everyone was so busy in the house that they did not see what was happening outside. The laborers were gathering on the lawn. They carried torches and baseball bats and crow bars. They began chanting, "Je chech."

"Is that French? What does it mean?"

"It is creole. The meaning seems harmless to someone not from the islands. The translation is *dry eyes*. The expression refers to someone who lies to your face about something bad they have done. Otto had done many bad things."

"Since he was so terrible, why was he not in jail?"

"Money buys many things... power, respect and freedom from responsibility for untoward actions. Money can even help you to get away with murder."

"Murder! Who did Otto murder?"

"Patience. All in good time."

After a moment, Lilian continued with her story.

"As the guests arrived, they were forced to push their way through the rioters. The foremen tried to enforce crowd control... tried to push the workers back to Bryant Village. Violence broke out.

Your father was watching from the front door. In the crowd,

Nicholas saw the young boy who had told him to lower his sail on the day he arrived in town. Do you know the story about your father's arrival?"

"Yes. Father called the boy Charlie. He told that story often… about being caught with the fishhook and dragged into the water. He always made it sound funny."

"Funny. Yes, I suppose in the retelling it could be a funny story. Your father wanted to meet Charlie, but he was elusive. No one seemed to know his name or where he lived or where he came from."

"That's impossible. This is a small town and he was just a child."

"Yes. Yes, he was, but what we know and what we choose to reveal are very different. A slip of the tongue, as they say, can lead to a noose being slipped around your neck."

"Who says that?"

"Helen, you are a breath of fresh air… a bit naive for a big city girl, but it is understandable. You are the wrong ethnicity to understand the connotation. Another day, I will explain. For now…

Fearing that the boy… Charlie… would be hurt if he remained among the rioters, Nicholas ran down the stairs, intending to scoop him up and bring him inside. Before he could reach him, Charlie ran away. Your father followed.

Out beyond the fields, beyond the tree line, was a barbed-wire-fence enclosed *No Trespassing* area. There was a gate, which was usually padlocked. Not that day. The gate was open, and Nicholas ran through, afraid that Charlie was in danger.

What he saw… it was a portent of things to come. Hidden by a dense forest of trees was a concrete pit. The pit was set deep into the ground. It was filled with water and alligators. Big alligators. Lots of them. Some of Otto Bryant's men were feeding them molasses.

"Why would anyone feed an alligator molasses?"

"As well as being naive, you are, obviously, not a farm girl. Molasses is a supplement given to livestock. It is an excellent source of minerals and provides a quick surge of energy, much like the energy drinks of today."

"So, if my father saw something very normal, why was it dangerous for him to be there?"

"It was dangerous for anyone to be there who was not employed by Mr. Bryant."

"What happened to Charlie?"

CHAPTER 14

"*We* can talk about Charlie later. Tell me about your mother."

"Most of my memories were created by my father. He painted pictures for me in the stories he told. He was so afraid I would forget her, but I have not.

I remember the scent of her perfume and the softness of her hair. Sometimes, when I am alone, I think I can feel her breath on the back of my neck, as if she is standing next to me. Sometimes, I hear her voice... the way she would sing me to sleep at night."

"My mother died when I was very young as well, Lillian said. "My father remarried and, luckily, my stepmother was a good woman. She loved me like her own." Lillian's face held more than a touch of regret.

"Did you love her?"

"Maybe. Probably. But, mostly, I just loved myself."

"That is a strange thing to say."

"I am a strange person. I tell fortunes... remember."

Irene Pierson met the handsome Nicholas Grant in 1980 when they were both copywriters for the Sarasota Herald-Tribune. Irene wanted to be an investigative reporter, as did Nicholas. Irene saw Nicholas as a rival. Nicholas found Irene's fighting spirit attractive. Her face and figure, both of which deserved to be on the cover of a fashion magazine, did not stifle his interest.

At the beginning of their relationship, they were adversaries. Later, they became frenemies, and soon after that, they became lovers. They were a formidable team, often working together to discover clues for unsolved murders in Sarasota County. They built a reputation for being bull dogs who, when they got their teeth into a story, did not stop searching until they had all the facts. Their award-winning articles were published under a joint by-line: The Pierson Grant Reports.

Irene was the granddaughter of the late Senator Everett Pierson from Massachusetts. Prior to his death at the age of 76, the Senator parlayed his granddaughter's and her soon-to-be husband's relative fame into a job at the prestigious Boston Globe. After their marriage in 1982, the newlyweds moved into a condo on Beacon Hill... the same condo which Helen had recently put up for sale after leaving her husband.

Irene and Nicholas were happy together, and their happiness increased when Irene discovered she was pregnant on their second wedding anniversary. Irene hoped for a daughter... a little girl she could dress in frilly outfits and with whom she could bake cookies. The maternal instinct grew stronger with each passing month.

Nicholas did not care about the gender of his child. He just wanted a baby who was healthy... a son or a daughter with whom he could build a relationship much like the one he had with his grandfather. His dearest wish was to love and be loved in return.

When Helen Pierson Grant was born with all her fingers and toes where they were supposed to be, Nicholas and Irene were ecstatic. Life was good. Until, it wasn't.

Helen was three years old when Irene discovered what she thought was a small blind pimple on her breast. She paid no attention to it until Nicholas mentioned that he felt a lump while they were making love. The pimple had grown into a cyst.

In the 1980s, a woman undergoing a biopsy for a breast tumor would remain on the operating table until the lump was examined. If cancer was found, an immediate radical mastectomy was performed. Radiation treatments followed, which sometimes damaged nearby organs, including the lungs. That is what happened to Irene.

The year following her mastectomy was one of dwindling good health. Although often too sick to get out of bed, she never ignored the needs of her daughter. She read her stories and sang her songs. On good days, they had tea parties and baked cookies.

On bad days, Nicholas became both mother and father. His relationship with Helen became deeper and stronger because he knew that soon it would be father and daughter against the world.

Just before Helen's fourth birthday, Irene died.

Nicholas was devastated, but his devotion to Helen kept him going. Every minute that he was not working, he spent preparing her for life's uncertain road. He did this by teaching her skills most little girls never acquired.

Helen learned to ride a horse, to sail a boat and to change the tire on a car. She could cook, sew and speak German, the language Nicholas' grandfather often spoke to him. Helen could read and write at a level far above her age by the time she was five. Often, over Sunday breakfast, a pre-teen Helen would read the stock market reports to her father and he, in turn, would explain how and why stocks were bought and sold.

Father and daughter shared every success and every failure. They laughed together and cried together. Nicholas instilled in Helen the desire to write by encouraging her to read the classics. Like her father, Helen idolized Hemingway and, because of the stories Nicholas told her every night at bedtime, she became an author of some celebrity by the time she was 25.

Every book she wrote carried the inscription, "To my father, without whom my life would have been very different. I love you!"

In March 2017, at the age of 69, Nicholas died of a sudden heart attack. That was five months ago. It wasn't until Helen went through the painful process of disposing of his worldly goods that she learned her father had a secret life. She had come to Pahokee to discover the truth about the man she thought she knew.

"I do not believe my mother knew anything about the time my father spent here. I never knew anything about it until he died. When his will was probated, I learned that he had left me two boats... the one in Boston and Typewriter. So, here I am."

CHAPTER 15

"*D*id my father and Rebecca ever get married?"

"No, but let's talk again in the morning. It is past mid-day, and I have anxious customers wanting to know their destinies. Coffee and donuts?"

"You know where to find me."

Much as her father had before her, Helen spent the day compiling notes on all that Lillian had told her. She found it difficult to believe that her father had loved a woman other than her mother. Yet, the more she searched the boat for clues to her father's past, the more the truth was revealed.

Stuffed in a slit on the underside of the bed mattress, Helen found photographs of Nicholas with a woman. Their arms were wrapped around each other in a loving embrace. The woman's face was blacked out; the force with which it was done leaving grooves in the picture. Had Nicholas blacked out the face? Had the woman?

Helen thought about the anger she felt for her husband and decided the woman, whom she believed was Rebecca, had destroyed the photos. Helen was angry that her husband had fallen in love with someone else. Perhaps, her father had fallen out of love with Rebecca. The reason the relationship ended was now added to the questions Helen needed to answer.

There was another picture in the pile, much different from the others. This one showed her father and a man she assumed was Otto Bryant kneeling next to a dead alligator. Otto Bryant held a shotgun. Nicholas was smiling but his smile seemed fake. Nicholas Grant had not been a hunter… not of people or animals.

Again, questions formed and Helen was determined to get answers. She put the photographs aside to show Lillian.

~

As day moved toward evening, Helen grew hungry. The fast food she had been subsisting on did not appeal to her. She decided to have dinner at the Grassy Waters Restaurant and Tiki Bar. A little music and a glass of wine was what she needed to calm her troubled spirits. Sitting at one of the outside tables, Helen was just beginning to relax when a man approached.

"Ms. Grant?"

"Yes?" Helen studied the man, who appeared to be in his seventies. His face was craggy, lined from years in the sun. His hair, what little there was of it, was gray and cut short, military style. "How can I help you?"

"May I sit a minute, ma'am. I have a story I would like to tell you."

"Seems everyone in Pahokee has a story to tell. Yes, sit down." As the man moved around the table to an empty chair, Helen noticed he had a slight limp.

"Allow me to introduce myself. My name is Sam Weatherby."

In his youth, Sam Weatherby had been a small-time hoodlum, who knew the inside of a prison cell better than he knew his own bedroom. He also knew Pahokee, and the stories he told gave Helen the answers to many of her questions. Those stories also filled her heart with fear. She knew she could not tell anyone, especially Lillian, what Sam had said. If she did, she might be running for her life just as her father had done four decades earlier.

~

"Your father was a bit of a Puritan, if I remember correctly." Lillian pried the top off her cup of take-out coffee and sipped the hot liquid carefully. "He had some kind of notion about women being pure as the driven snow. Historically, that has never been a realistic expectation and, certainly, not where Rebecca was concerned."

"Was she a wanton woman?"

"No. Not exactly. She was more of a renegade. She believed females should have the same rights as men. She lived her life by her own rules."

"I can see my father breaking the engagement if he felt Rebecca did not live up to his idea of the perfect woman."

"I think she knew that as well."

"My father mellowed as he aged. When I turned 16, he talked to me about how expectations and perceptions were two different things. He said that feminists had expectations of what it meant to be liberated but that the sexual revolution had centuries of bias to overcome."

"What message was he trying to convey?"

"That, while he recognized that times had changed, society had not necessarily kept up with those changes. He always said it was impossible to erase a first impression."

"Did he expect you to remain a virgin until you got married?"

"My virginal state was never up for discussion. I am pretty sure he knew that sainthood was not in my future."

"I have always found it interesting that what men say and what men do are as different as apples and artichokes."

"Don't you mean oranges?"

"No. What a man says and what a man does when it comes to women and sex is far more different than apples and oranges."

"So, you are saying that even if my father knew that Rebecca was not a virgin, he would have married her."

"Yes. I think so, but I do not believe Rebecca was willing to take that chance."

"Would she have killed to keep her secret?"

"What a strange question to ask! I, honestly, do not know."

"What kind of a fortune teller are you, anyway." Helen laughed but her laughter had a hollow sound to it.

CHAPTER 16

"*Where* did you find these?"

"In a slit on the underside of the mattress."

Lillian held each picture as though it was a precious jewel. "They were very happy together... your father and Rebecca. What a shame that someone blackened her face."

"I think she did it."

"Maybe."

"Who is the man in the photo with the alligator? Is it Otto Bryant?"

Lillian stared at the picture; disdain written on her face. "Yes. That's Otto. No doubt that alligator became a pair of boots, a belt, a wallet, and maybe even a seat cover for his office chair. Otto both loved and hated those escapees from Jurassic Park.

I remember Rebecca telling me about a party Otto held to celebrate her and Nicholas' coming nuptials. The liquor flowed and everyone got drunk. In the morning, Otto told Nicholas to load the leftovers into the back of a pickup truck.

The three of them drove out into the backwater... the private area beyond the cane fields where Otto had the alligator pen. The man was obsessed with their skins.

Anyway, when they got there, Otto backed the truck up to the pond and told Nicholas to throw the food into the water. There was a feeding frenzy. So many gators, snapping and hissing.

Otto thrived on violence. Rebecca told me her father made a comment about how the alligators would tear a man to shreds in seconds given the chance. She said your dad was standing in the truck bed, and Otto caused the truck to rock back and forth. Your father near died of fright. Otto thought it was hilarious. He told the story to anyone who would listen."

"I have no reason not to believe you."

~

Sam Weatherby moved around the table and took the seat next to Helen.

"Would you like something to eat or drink?"

"No, thank you. I just need to talk.

You might have noticed that I walk with a limp. Happened years ago. I told everyone that I tripped while carrying a window and put my foot through the glass. There was no reason for anyone not to believe me.

The truth… the truth is that Otto Bryant tried to kill me to keep me from talking about his family. He always wore an alligator belt with a big brass buckle. I did not know that the buckle was actually a case for a three-inch knife that was so sharp it could take the hide off a buffalo. Good thing I was quick with my fists, or I would not be here talking to you."

"Why had you come to Pahokee, Mr. Weatherby?"

To see my mother, Eloise Weatherby. The Bryant's housekeeper and cook."

~

Eloise Weatherby, nee Addington, was born in St. Bernard Parish, Louisiana on April 15, 1927. It was Good Friday. It was also the day 15 inches of rain fell in New Orleans in 18 hours. Two weeks later, the city government decided to dynamite the levee in Caenarvon with the intent of sparing New Orleans serious damage from overflowing rivers.

The loss of the levee resulted in 250,000 cubic feet of water being released upon the Addington family's homestead. Eloise and her parents barely escaped. They had only the clothes on their backs and a few dollars in a coffee can stuffed in a pillowcase.

The Great Mississippi Flood of 1927 killed 500 people. Hundreds of thousands of survivors lived in relief camps while waiting for government help, which never came. Eloise took her first steps in a mud floor tent with only one cot upon which mother, father and baby slept. Life was tough, but Eloise was tougher.

CHAPTER 17

"*G*et out before I slit your throat."

"You don't scare me, Otto. Everyone else in this town might be afraid of you, but I'm not. If you kill me, you will have a rebellion on your hands, and those secrets you are so desperate to keep… well, they will be front page news all over the state."

Otto Bryant was not an easily intimidated man but, then again, neither was Sam Weatherby. Years in prison had toughened him both mentally and physically. He was a survivor, a survivor who was very comfortable using blackmail as a means to an end.

"You best be treating my mother well… paying her well… paying her enough so that she can help her loving son, who is struggling financially since being released from the pen.

How much money have you got in your wallet, Otto? I will bet it is a bundle. Just hand it over, and I will be out of your way."

"You piece of shit. The only thing I will hand over to you is your head."

Otto rushed Sam, but being younger and more physically fit, Sam was able to dodge and weave until he grabbed Otto in a head lock. What Sam did not know was that Otto had a few moves of his own. He reached for the knife hidden in his belt buckle and stabbed Sam hard in the thigh, just missing the femoral artery.

Eloise, who had been watching the confrontation from the hallway, screamed and ran to help her son. Otto backed away, wiping the knife on the sleeve of his shirt.

"Get him out of here, Eloise."

Otto took a roll of cash from his pocket and threw it at Sam. "This is all you are getting. Pay Doc Dozier to stitch you up and use the rest to get out of town. Keep your mouth shut."

As Otto left the room, he turned to Eloise. "And that goes for you, too. I have been patient, but I will not be for much longer."

Eloise was on her hands and knees cleaning blood off the rug when Sandra and Rebecca entered. They had been shopping for Rebecca's honeymoon trousseau and were giddy from the champagne they had enjoyed with their lunch.

"Eloise…" Sandra, surprised at seeing Eloise on the floor, nearly choked on her laughter. "What are you doing?"

"It's nothing, Mrs. Bryant. One of the dogs caught a raccoon. He got in the house somehow and dragged it all over the carpet. I will be out of here in a minute."

"Those dogs… they are a menace. I am grateful you weren't bitten."

"They are watch dogs, Momma. Menacing is their least terrifying quality."

Rebecca stood at the bar, a decanter of scotch in her hands. "Shall we have another?"

As she turned her back to pour, Rebecca's hands began to shake. She was not fooled by Eloise' explanation. Something had happened. Something very, very bad. Her intuition told her that Sam was involved.

Richard Dozier had been the only doctor in Pahokee for going on 50 years. He had opened his office fresh out of medical school. From birth to death, it was his name on the certificates attesting to parentage and cause of demise. He knew a lot but said little. When he did talk, it was because he feared *more of the same* or worse would be crossing his doorstep.

When Sam Weatherby hobbled back to his car that fateful day, Doc Dozier called Deputy Lamont Minor. The wheels of destiny had been set in motion.

Several hours later, there was an urgent knock on the Bryant family's front door. Eloise answered. Seeing Lamont and another deputy, her face turned a lighter shade of pale.

"Good evening, Eloise. If you have a moment, I would like to speak with you."

Otto joined Eloise in the vestibule. He exchanged pleasantries with Lamont and the deputy as though their visit had been expected. What followed was an academy award winning performance by two people trying to keep the truth from being known but not having a clue how to do that.

When Lamont asked Eloise if she was aware that her son was in town and that he had been injured, Otto answered for her. She did not know. She could not know. She had been working all day. Being a considerate employer, Otto told Eloise to leave immediately and tend to her son.

Lamont bid Eloise and Otto good night. Despite being told nothing he did not already know; he had all the answers he needed.

CHAPTER 18

*N*icholas, who was having dinner with the Bryants that night, was not fooled by Otto's explanation when he returned to the table. Should he have needed further proof that Otto was lying - which he did not - it could be found on Rebecca's face. If fear needed a visual, a photograph taken of her at that very moment would have served perfectly.

Whatever romantic yearnings Nicholas felt at the beginning of the evening were quashed by the physical and emotional distance Rebecca put between them when dinner was over. She was jittery, so much so that she could not sit still for more than a few minutes. She was also drinking to excess, barely finishing one glass of scotch before pouring another.

With conversation at a standstill, Nicholas bid good night to Otto and Sandra, kissed Rebecca on the cheek, and left. The seeds of distrust had been planted and, when they sprouted, they would bring with them a harvest of hurt like nothing he had ever known.

An hour later, Nicholas was standing on deck, looking out at the horizon, when he heard a voice behind him. "What's that saying, 'Troubles by day. Troubles by night. Troubles will give you one hell of a fright.'"

Lamont stood on the pier, holding a bottle of wine and two glasses in his hand.

"Never heard that saying. I am partial to 'Drink enough wine and your troubles will be forgotten.' If that bottle is for me, come on board."

While their friendship was new, the respect these two men felt for each other was evident in the grip of their handshake. They did not speak, each trying to decide the best way to approach a topic that was both sensitive and explosive. For the moment, the clinking of glasses and the sipping of wine were enough.

"Why did you come to the house tonight?"

Lamont poured the last few drops of wine into his glass as he answered. "What did Otto tell you?"

"Lies. From you, I expect the truth no matter what that truth might be."

"That is the problem. I only think I know the truth. I don't have any proof."

"Then tell me what you think. I will find out the truth for myself."

Neither man saw bed that night. They talked as the moon rose and set in the sky.

The sun was barely up when Nicholas and Lamont drove to the boarding house where Sam Weatherby was staying. They pounded on the door to Sam's room but to no avail. Lamont used a well-placed foot to kick the door in.

The room was a mess. The bed had been turned upside down. The dresser drawers were pulled out and the contents scattered about the floor. Chair cushions were split open. The discount store paintings that should have been hanging on the wall were ripped from their frames and tossed aside.

There were plenty of signs that Sam Weatherby had lived there, but there was no Sam Weatherby. Hours of driving around town, turned up no clues. Sam was gone, and Lamont and Nicholas were convinced he had not left willingly.

Nicholas was determined to confront Otto and Rebecca. He wanted answers and he wanted them quickly.

He and Lamont returned to the marina to find Sugar Wrench waiting on the dock. Noth had been seriously hurt while repairing a leak in the underside of a 12-foot motorboat. The lift had let go, bringing the full weight of the boat down on Noth, crushing his pelvis. He was in the hospital, fighting for his life.

Nicholas' forgot all about Otto and Rebecca. He considered Noth and Roosevelt good friends. The brothers had been there for him when he needed help. Now, he needed to be there for them.

CHAPTER 19

*R*oosevelt and Noth Chosen were minor celebrities from the moment they popped out of the womb. Roosevelt was older by two minutes. He weighed 12.6 pounds. Noth was smaller. He weighed only 12 pounds. Both screamed their arrival, making sure their mother knew she would have her work cut out for her.

The boys looked identical right down to the Mongolian spot birthmark on the left cheek of their buttocks. They each had a full head of hair and slept with their eyes partially open. So that no mistakes would be made in the hospital nursery, one of their aunts sewed tee shirts with the words "Roo" and "Noth" embroidered on the front. That's how Roosevelt got his nickname. Being called "The Chosen Ones" came later.

Roo and Noth were good babies... active but good. When they slept, they slept soundly. When they ate, their appetites were impressive. They smiled all the time and were amenable to being held by anyone who could handle their hefty size. They grew quickly, gaining a pound and growing an inch a week. When they were nine months old, Doc Dozier's scale registered an impressive 30 pounds each.

The brothers, who were inseparable from the day they were born, took their first steps together. They spoke their first word - "eat" - just moments apart. They liked and disliked the same foods. Burgers and fries were their favorites; with liver and onions being on the "no no" list.

School was a challenge... for the teachers, not the brothers. They received the same high grades on every test no matter the subject. Any incorrect answers were the same incorrect answers whether the test was for math, grammar, history or geography.

Their teachers were convinced that the boys were cheating off each other's papers, so they sat them at desks on opposite sides of the classroom. Roosevelt sat near the teacher's desk and Noth sat in the rear near the coat closet. The results were the same.

Needless to say, the brothers excelled at sports. Both were right-handed, although they bowled lefty. They were always the high scorers on their intramural team. In high school, they were star football players with Roosevelt playing left offensive guard and Noth playing right offensive guard. For four years, they shared the most valuable player trophy, having led their team in winning the state championships.

During their senior year, both brothers broke their left arm on the same play during the final game of the season. The breaks were in exactly the same place. Their casts were removed on the same day and the brothers were back in the bowling alley that night.

Upon graduation from high school, the boys went into business together. Noth was a commercial fisherman with an extensive knowledge of boats and boat engines. Roosevelt could repair a car or truck engine with his eyes closed. They called their company *The Chosen Ones* and credited the same aunt who had made their tee shirts with coming up with the idea. Being well liked and having a reputation as hard workers, they were an immediate success.

Since the brothers did everything together, vacations were no exception. On a fishing trip to Georgia, they met identical twin sisters, fell in love and married within a few months. The two couples shared not just a house; they shared their lives.

On the way to a celebratory first anniversary dinner, a car driven by a drunk driver ran a red light. The impact was so powerful that the sisters were thrown from the car and died at the scene. Noth and

Roosevelt, being so heavy, remained in their seats. Both had a concussion and a broken nose, but other than that, they were unharmed. While their physical injuries were minor, the emotional turmoil was double what it would have been for anyone else.

Being of one mind, Roosevelt and Noth did not need to speak to know what the other was thinking. They felt each other's pain and, on the day the boat came crashing down on Noth, Roosevelt walked with a noticeable tilt to one side, as if he had broken his hip.

The tears on his face were real. He did not try to hide them. When he looked at his brother lying in the hospital bed, he saw himself. If Noth died, Roosevelt knew he would not be far behind.

CHAPTER 20

*W*hen Roosevelt, Nicholas and Lamont arrived at the hospital, Sadie Mae was keeping vigil at Noth's bedside. X-rays had shown that the breaks to both sides of Noth's pelvis were not as severe as originally thought. Doctors had performed emergency surgery, whereby they inserted metal pins to repair the areas between the femoral heads and the femoral necks. Months of recovery and physical therapy lay ahead, but Noth would walk again.

To say that Roosevelt was relieved would be an understatement. He had been prepared to care for his brother no matter what that entailed and, with the help of his friends and his niece, the job would not have been overwhelming. He would be able to continue working and serving both his own customers and his brother's clients.

"Doc Dozier is giving me every Friday off and letting me work half days Monday through Thursday. And, he is paying me my full salary, too. I will be able help you, Uncle Roo, so don't worry." Sadie Mae hugged her uncle and wiped the tears from his face.

"I'll be there to help, too," Lamont assured his friend.

"And me, too," Nicholas joined in. "I do not know much about engines, but I can be your gofer."

While Nicolas was patting Roosevelt reassuringly on the back, he was also thinking that now he had a good excuse for snooping around and asking questions. And, he would start by finding out what happened to Sam Weatherby.

~

Almost 48 hours had passed since Nicholas had felt a mattress under his back. He was exhausted when Lamont dropped him back at the marina. No sooner had he climbed on board than Rebecca appeared, crying a torrent of tears in apology for her behavior. Holding her in his arms... cradling her head against his shoulder... Nicholas felt all his resolve drain away. He loved her. He was willing to believe whatever she said, even if deep down inside he knew they were half-truths or outright lies.

~

Nicholas Grant knew little of Rebecca's heritage. What he did know was based on assumptions. Bryant was an old Irish surname derived from the Celtic for the first name Brion. Upon meeting Otto Bryant, Rebecca's father, Nicholas assumed the man to be of German/Irish descent. Otto seemed like a fitting first name for a man who had acquired vast wealth. Otto meant "wealthy" in German.

Otto's second wife, Sandra, had all the markings of an Irish lass... fair skin, a scattering of freckles across her nose, red hair and green eyes. Nicholas had no idea, nor did he care what her maiden name had been. She was sassy, smart and married to the man who had sired the love of his life. Rebecca!

Nicholas Grant was a man who accepted people at face value when first meeting them. He believed in trusting the people he loved until they gave him reason not to. He believed that his idol, Ernest Hemingway, had it right when he said, "The best way to find out if you can trust somebody is to trust them."

Where the Bryants were concerned, Nicholas would soon find out the error in Hemingway's manner of thinking.

Although Nicholas had been barely able to put one foot in front of the other when he arrived back at the boat, the mere sight of Rebecca had filled him with renewed energy. He could not keep himself from touching her face, her hair, and running his fingers across her lips. He did that even while she was talking and, eventually, she took to playfully biting them in a somewhat suggestive way. Nicholas took the hint. He picked Rebecca up and carried her to the cabin.

The sounds of frantic lovemaking turned to sighs of satisfaction and, in time, were replaced by the slow, regular breathing of two people sleeping contentedly. Nicholas forgot the wounds and worries that had been festering and growing in his heart and mind the past few days. Rebecca was in his arms and all was right with the world.

CHAPTER 21

$\mathcal{F}$or decades, the chief supplier of labor in Florida's sugar cane fields has been the Caribbean islands. Eight to nine thousand men and women normally constitute what is the largest legal foreign migrant labor force in the United States.

Growing sugar in Florida is a precarious and competitive business. Unlike most other states that produce sugar, Florida relies almost exclusively on manual harvesting. Government regulations require that employers offer their workers an hourly wage in excess of prevailing agricultural rates. They also receive living accommodations, meals and transportation, all of which the workers pay for.

Due to the low wages and high unemployment in the Caribbean, the demand for jobs in Florida far exceeds the need for workers. This allows unscrupulous employers to take advantage of the desperate need for money inherent in field help. Workers flown in from the islands are already in debt as they must reimburse their government for the expense of the flight.

Harvesting sugar cane is labor intensive and dirty. The hot Florida sun turns the workers skin to an animal-hide-like texture and damages eyesight. Injuries are a common occurrence as the machetes used to cut the canes are extremely sharp. Sugar cane workers often experience kidney damage and respiratory issues. Employers are legally allowed to require an eight-hour day, six days a week with a 15-minute break for lunch. The average number of hours worked is much higher since no one is monitoring the industry.

Life in Bryant Village and in the fields at the Bryant Sugar Mill relied heavily on the oversight of supervisors. Jamaicans tended to hold the majority of supervisory positions and, while all workers were meant to be treated equally, the predominance of Jamaicans in charge was often a source of complaint. The magnitude of bias was proportionate to a worker's place of birth.

Otto Bryant spent his formative years in the no-man's land between the black and white races. His father was what white slave owners once called an octoroon, meaning he was one eighth black. His mother was a hexadecaroon, meaning she was one-sixteenth black. For all intents and purposes, Otto's parents were white but *civilized* society still saw them as inferior.

To the white race, one drop of black blood was all it took to make Otto black. To the black race, he was white and, based on the actual color of his skin, they were correct. He was a man without a race, a place and a country.

The ethnic roadblocks constantly in his way made Otto hard. His unsuccessful attempt to be seen as an individual not a skin color made him angry. When the opportunity arose for him to buy a struggling sugar cane farm, he took it. In time, he became was one of the most successful sugar cane growers in south Florida.

In an industry dominated by white men, Otto Bryant knew that passing himself and his family off as white was necessary to survive a socially hostile environment. He hid the truth of his heritage with a fierceness that, when threatened, allowed him to commit inhumane acts beyond that which even the Devil could imagine.

Otto Bryant went from near poverty to great wealth in the span of a few decades. He was a tyrant; a man who manipulated the laws that were in place to protect workers and pay them a fair salary. Field help was guaranteed a minimum hourly wage based on the expectation that they would cut an average of eight tons of cane a day. Otto paid them half the expected rate. Rarely did anyone complain. The punishment was too great.

CHAPTER 22

*S*adie Mae was a godsend to her Uncle Roosevelt. She was as efficient as any nurse and provided that extra tender-loving touch that Noth needed during his recovery and rehabilitation. With Sadie on call, Roosevelt was able to carry the burden of running two businesses.

When Lamont was off duty, he spent hours putting his high school vocational training to good use. He had loved automotive shop and was good at handling the *normal* everyday mechanics of a truck or car engine. Spark plugs, batteries and oil changes were his specialty. The more advanced repairs were handled by Roosevelt personally.

The same held true for boat engines, although Lamont was inclined to let Roosevelt handle the big and the small boat problems by himself. Despite growing up on the shores of Lake Okeechobee, no one would ever have referred to him as a "water rat." Lamont liked his feet firmly planted on hard ground.

While Rebecca was working at the mill, Nicholas spent his time running errands for Roosevelt. The Original Equipment Company, a small family-owned and operated automotive distributor of car parts was located in Belle Glade, a 40-minute round trip from Pahokee. Nicholas made the drive, using Roosevelt's old pickup truck, at least twice a week. He picked up the mail every day and went to the grocery store whenever necessary.

Each of these chores put Nicholas in a position to get to know the locals on a first-name basis. The more they saw him, they more they trusted him. The more they trusted him, the loser their lips became when talking about the Bryant family.

Within a few short weeks, the residents of Pahokee had taken a proprietary stance when it came to Nicholas' relationship with Rebecca. They liked him. They did not like her. Very quickly, the old worries and doubts, which Nicholas had pushed to the back of his mind, resurfaced, and this time, they came back with a vengeance.

The grocery story, owned by Otto Bryant, was the center of the town in two important ways… its location and its appeal as a gathering place for field workers and residents alike. Pahokee was already a small town where everyone knew everyone. The store was gossip central; the place where secrets were revealed and information was traded for a price.

During one shopping excursion, Nicholas heard someone singing, and the song got louder as the person singing it drew closer.

> *What was in store, I did not know.*
> *She waved me on, so I had to go.*
> *She gave me love, oh yes, so much,*
> *A helpless fool at her tender touch.*

A Haitian woman, the one he thought of as the Vodou priestess, came toward him. Not until their noses practically touched did she stop moving. In a new voice, this one barely above a whisper and having a tone so chilling that it sent shivers down Nicholas' spine, she said, "The answers to all your questions are in their eyes. Do not close your own or you will be blinded to the truth. The one you seek is hiding in the village."

As the woman moved away, she began singing her song again. Nicholas was held still and silent by shock. Before he could form a response... before her words had taken on their true meaning... she was gone. He hurried through the store looking for her, but she was nowhere to be found.

CHAPTER 23

"When I was a little girl, my father would hum a song with a calypso beat. He told me he learned it from a Vodou priestess. Of course, I knew he was teasing me."

"What makes you so sure?" Lillian began to laugh when she saw the surprised look on Helen's face.

"Remember, the people who worked in the sugar cane fields were from the Caribbean. Calypso was their standard of music. Your father heard many songs when he visited Rebecca at the mill."

Helen began to hum the melody as she remembered it from her childhood. "Do you know the words, Lillian?"

"No. The workers usually sang in their native patois, which was difficult for anyone not from the islands to understand."

"Did you ever meet a man by the name of Carl Newsom? My dad said he was a good friend but that he caused a lot of trouble."

"I heard stories. Carl is the reason your father and Lamont eventually became friends. The beginning of their relationship was a bit criminal, you might say."

~

Carl Newsom was an old friend of Nicholas from his high school days. They kept in touch over the years, mostly through Christmas cards and the occasional phone call. How Carl found out about Nicholas' boat trip to Pahokee was a mystery, but one sunny day, he cruised into the marina parking lot driving a brand-new bright orange Z28 Camaro. That car was an instant attention getter.

Nicholas was happy to see a familiar face and excited to ride in a car known for going from stop to "Holy shit!" in seconds. The local police did not share his enthusiasm.

With Newsom closing in on 100 mph, they took a joy ride which left a cloud of dust in their wake. On State Road 715, they passed Lamont in his patrol car. Lights flashing and siren screaming, Lamont gave chase. He caught up to the Camaro, forcing Carl to the side of the road.

The sound of Lamont's boots pounding the roadway as he approached the car had Carl and Nicholas laughing, until they saw his face. They knew there was no way they would talk themselves out of a ticket or jail, for that matter.

After calling for a tow truck, Lamont handcuffed Carl and Nicholas and put them in the back of his car. Sunlight could be seen flaring off the Camaro as he drove back to town.

"Rebecca came to their rescue," Lillian continued with her story. "After an uncomfortable night in a small cell, she was able to bail them out. The Bryant name held sway with every elected official in the county.

Carl's visit to Pahokee lasted only a few days. Every morning when he and Nicholas awoke, they would find Lamont sitting in his patrol car in the marina parking lot. He always chose the spot next to the Camaro, which had been towed to the marina at a cost of $500.

If Nicholas and Carl drove anywhere in the car, Lamont was close behind them. His presence took all the fun out of having a muscle car.

On the day that Carl left, Lamont followed him to the city line and waved goodbye as he crossed over into Belle Glade.

Nicholas knew it was in his best interests to apologize to Lamont for his part in Carl's reckless driving stunt. He stopped by the police station and, with all humility, offered to pay the ticket that Otto Bryant had gotten squashed.

Lamont was impressed with his sincerity. Since he did not have the authority to take money for a ticket that did not exist, the two men decided to have lunch together with Nicholas paying the bill. A friendship was born over fried catfish and hush puppies.

CHAPTER 24

*L*oyalty ran strong in Lamont Minor's blood... loyalty to his African heritage, loyalty to his family, loyalty to his hometown of Pahokee and loyalty to his badge. His great great grandfather and grandmother had been among the first blacks to move to the area in the early 1900s to work on the farms that grew most of the fresh produce for the east coast. Generation after generation of Minors had carried on that tradition, never expecting more out of life than enough money to keep a roof over their heads and food on the table. That changed when Lamont was born.

Like all parents, Lamont's mother and father wanted more for their son. They made sure he never missed a day of school and always got good grades. Even after his parents divorced and his father moved a few miles away, he remained a major influence on Lamont.

The senior Minor knew that if his son was ever to get out of The Glades, he would need to play football, and he would need to play well. Every weekend, he drilled Lamont on the finer points of the game. While other little boys were catching bugs, Lamont was running laps and learning how to tackle.

By the time he was 13, Lamont was tall and lanky - just under six foot and weighing 150 pounds. All the years of running around his backyard while his father timed his efforts had paid off. He was fast! He could complete the 40-yard dash in 4.6 seconds. Along with the Chosen brothers, who were two years older, Lamont Minor was thought to be headed for stardom.

In his senior year of high school, scouts from major league teams came calling, but much to his father's disappointment, Lamont was not interested. He had quietly harbored another dream since he was a little boy. He wanted to work in law enforcement.

During a second-grade social studies class, Lamont learned about Samuel Battle, the first black police officer in New York City. He eventually became the NYPD's first black sergeant, first black lieutenant and first black parole commissioner. Lamont idolized him.

While disappointed that one of his star players was not interested in a career on the gridiron, his coach recognized that Lamont was college material. He worked a miracle and got him a scholarship to Florida State, where he earned a Bachelor of Science degree and maintained a 3.8 grade point average all four years. Upon graduation, despite having offers to work in the state capital, he returned to Pahokee. Loyalty made the decision easy.

Whenever Lamont was asked why he had decided to return home, he would talk about how every day during history class, he would look out the window and see former Blue Devil star players loitering in front of the school. They had been great players at the high school level, but not great enough to make it in the Big Leagues. These young men, who had been singularly focused on sports, had no jobs and no futures. Crime was their career.

Sam Battle had worked with hundreds of young men just like these. He had started rehabilitation programs and sports camps to help the youth of Harlem. Lamont dreamed of doing much the same for Pahokee.

~

"Other than using my town as the southern terminus for the Daytona

500, what are you doing here?" Lamont poked a little fun at Nicholas as they ate their lunch.

"Not sure, yet. Pahokee was not on my itinerary. I guess you could say that fate had other plans for me... fate and a cracked distributor cap."

"Hmmm. And now that the boat is fixed?"

"I met a girl..."

"Yeah. So, I heard. How do you feel about working with troubled youths?"

"I... No. Wait. Is this because of the speeding ticket? I... I am buying you lunch. I do not owe you anything. I mean..."

Nicholas knew he had been outsmarted. Lamont smiled and continued to eat his lunch. The catfish was especially good that day.

CHAPTER 25

*C*uriosity finally got the better of Nicholas and he set out to find Charlie or, at least, someone who would talk to him about Charlie. Surprisingly, there wasn't anybody… at first.

Most people would just shake their heads or shrug their shoulders as if to say, "I do not know anyone by that name." Others would do an about face and quickly walk away. The more people professed ignorance; the more Nicholas was determined to learn everything there was to know. The one trait every person had in common… they were scared.

As Nicholas walked the streets of Pahokee, a quote by Julius Caesar played on automatic rewind in his head.

"No one is so brave that he is not disturbed by something unexpected."

Disturbed. Maybe that was a better word than scared. The people Nicholas spoke to seemed disturbed by his questions and he, in turn, felt uneasy with their avoidance of a response.

The unexpected came in the form of a familiar face. Sadie Mae sauntered down main street, a strained smile on her face.

"Nicholas, I hear you are asking questions about Charlie."

"So, you admit there is a Charlie. I was beginning to think I was living in the Twilight Zone."

"Come with me."

Sadie's car was parked behind the general store. She motioned for Nicholas to get in and quickly headed out of town. Nicholas recognized the road as the same one he had driven to reach Bryant Sugar.

As the entrance to the mill's main parking lot came into view, Sadie turned to the left and took a road that led around the sugar cane fields. Eventually, she stopped in front of one of the nicer houses in Bryant Village.

For the first time in his life, Nicholas knew what it meant to be the lone man out. He was the only white face in the crowd that was growing around Sadie Mae's car. As the people pressed closer to him, he had a moment of deja vu. Someone was singing the song he had heard on the day he toured the field with Rebecca and Otto. It was the same song... the same voice as the woman who had approached him in the grocery store.

"Why do I get the feeling that song is meant for me?"

"She is reciting a poem set to music about a treacherous woman from the islands."

"For my benefit?"

"Perhaps. Do you know what Vodou is, Nicholas?"

"Sure. It's the religion of the Caribbean islands. Zombies and dead people rising."

"That is Hollywood's version of Vodou. There are no zombies... no dead people walking the earth. Vodou is a union between believers and the divine spirits which live inside each one of us. That union is achieved through communal rituals like the beating of drums, dancing and singing."

"So, is that song a prayer being said for me?"

"Not for you but to you... to warn you."

"Can you translate?"

"Yes.

I went down to the Caribbean Sea,
an island paradise ahead of me.
I meant to go for just another lay,
so I went and got myself smashed that day.

Saw her standing there, with coal black eyes,
and long dark hair, that didn't disguise,
the curves she had, caught me off guard
she was the finest thing down in that bar.

As I drew up near, my ride began,
I should've feared that Creole woman.

What was in store, I did not know.
she waved me on, so I had to go.
She gave me love, oh yes, so much,
a helpless fool at her tender touch.

A night gone by, the best I ever had,
the kind of lover who drove men mad.
As morning came, I thanked sweet God,
but she was gone, and I was robbed.

I stumbled out onto the sand,
I cursed her name, Creole woman.

My passport she left, that one small gift,
the cops said she'd given the many the shrift.
The tropical waves lost their attraction,
I hopped a plane, got back to Jackson.

It started soon, the identity thieving,
had to fight every step, the stress unceasing.
A lesson learned, but which still does vex,
the things that woman can do with sex.

Next time I vacation in Japan,
far as I can get from Creole woman.[1]

"Sounds rather silly, don't you think?"

"I think the old woman has seen much and knows much. You would be wise not to ignore her. And, her name is Edeline. Remember it."

---

1. Caribbean Woman by David Welch

CHAPTER 26

When the Haitian woman's song came to an end, the crowd that had gathered around Nicholas and Sadie parted. No longer was Nicholas the only white face in Bryant Village. Eloise Weatherby stood before him, holding the hand of a small boy who could be none other than Charlie.

One look at his eyes and Nicholas knew why Rebecca refused to talk about this child. One half of his parentage was clearly written on his face. The other half, as well as the how, what, when and why of his birth, still needed to be discovered.

❧

Charlie Weatherby was four years shy of becoming a teenager. He was a beautiful boy in an exotic way. His skin was the color of coffee with a heavy pouring of milk. His hair was the yellow of fresh corn and hung in long, loose curls around his heart-shaped face. He had light, topaz-colored eyes, long dark eyelashes, and full lips. His teeth were small luminescent pearls. The only facial feature which belied his heritage was his nose, which was short and slender at the bridge widening at the tip and becoming splayed at the nostrils.

Charlie was big for his age and reed thin. His hands and feet were oversized, a sign that he would be tall and strong as an adult. He moved with the speed of a jackrabbit... there one minute and gone the next. The field workers referred to him as The Wind, swearing they could feel a soft breeze whenever he was near.

Being mentally challenged, Charlie preferred silence to speech unless absolutely necessary. He was a rarity in the medical world; someone who was both blessed and cursed. The curse was being born to a mother who tossed him around like a rag doll, causing severe head trauma to the left anterior temporal lobe. He was blessed to have had a grandmother who loved him and took charge of his care. Sadly, his grandmother could do nothing to reverse the brain injury, which resulted in Charlie having savant syndrome.

Nicholas approached Charlie carefully.

"Hello, Charlie. I'm Nicholas. I have been wanting to thank you for helping me with my boat."

Charlie's eyes grew wide. No doubt, he remembered hurting Nicholas with the fishhook and was afraid he would be punished.

"I am not angry with you. The fishhook was an accident. I know that. I would like us to be friends."

Charlie remained quiet, continuing to hold onto Eloise's hand. He studied Nicholas' face, looking for signs that he was lying, but all he saw was kindness. Once he accepted that Nicholas was someone who truly wanted to be his friend, he let go of Eloise and stepped forward.

"You put up the sail."

Nicholas and Sadie spent the next two hours with grandmother and grandson. Little by little, the pieces of the jigsaw puzzle fit together; and the picture those pieces created was not flattering for the Bryant family.

91

"Did you know about Charlie's parents, Sadie Mae?"

"Suspected."

"You should have told me."

"You would not have believed me, Nicholas. You needed to see Charlie with your own eyes."

CHAPTER 27

Since the Bryant Sugar Mill was only a few miles from Bryant Village, Nicholas asked Sadie Mae to drop him there. Rebecca would be working, and he was determined to speak to her.

When they arrived, pandemonium reigned. Black smoke poured from the mill, creating a cloud so dense and dark that sight was impaired and breathing was difficult. The cloud hung heavy over the mill and office, blocking out the sun. Flames shot out of the structure to a height of 10 feet.

A frantic Rebecca stood next to her father, who was screaming at the mill workers to get more hoses and put out the blaze. Nicholas and Sadie rushed to Rebecca's side. So focused was she on her father that, at first, she did not notice them. When Nicholas put his hand on her shoulder, she turned and fell in his arms, tears running down her face.

"What happened?"

"The sugar dust exploded. There must have been a spark from one of the machines or someone lit a match."

"Sugar explodes?" Nicholas' voice was filled with confusion.

"Yes. It has happened before, but never like this."

Seeing Nicholas standing with Rebecca, Otto came toward him, burnt sugar soot and sweat on his face and clothing. "Nicholas, thank God you are here. Take Rebecca away from this place. It's not safe."

"Is there something I can do to help?"

"No. No. Just keep my little girl safe."

With Sadie at the wheel, the threesome drove toward town. Engines from the Canal Point Battalion 7 Fire Department came roaring toward them, forcing Sadie to pull to the side of the road.

"I hope they get there in time." Rebecca's voice was soft, as if she was praying.

Nicholas held Rebecca's hand tightly. "Tell me what happened."

"Everyone thinks sugar is a benign product. It's sweet. It tastes good. How dangerous could it be?

The truth is that stirring sugar into your coffee is one thing. Making sugar is another. Dust from any organic material can burn."

"Like what?"

"Dust from grains and wood. All you need are the right conditions. Think of it this way. If I was baking a cake, which I would never do, but if I was, and I used powdered sugar, the air would be filled with the dust from the sugar. That dust is made of millions of sugar molecules - carbon, hydrogen and oxygen atoms - linked together. When carbon gets hot, it burns.

Sugar dust is made during the last stage of processing. Crystals are poured through a heated dryer to remove whatever moisture is left. The refined sugar is placed on a conveyer belt and moved to a silo for storage. Moving the sugar causes dust to float into the air. A spark from anything - a motor, a pump, a light switch - can set off an explosion. If the fire gets into the silo, the flames have an endless source of energy. Temperatures can reach over 4,000 degrees Fahrenheit."

"Holy shit!"

"What's going to happen to the mill?" Sadie had not spoken up to this point, so intent was she in listening to Rebecca's recitation.

"The workers saw the fire quickly and, while it looked bad from the outside, I think we will sustain minimal damage. But minimal means part of the mill will be shut down for a few months. That is going to hurt our bottom line. We have outstanding orders that need to be filled. Our customers can get irate if their demands are not met on time."

"How do you think the fire started?" Sadie looked over her shoulder at Rebecca. She and Nicholas were in the backseat and sitting so close together as to be one person.

"I have no idea, but if my father finds out it was human error, there will be a feast at the alligator pit tomorrow night."

Nicholas's and Sadie Mae's eyes met in the rearview mirror. Their unspoken question - "What does that mean?" - hung uncomfortably between them.

CHAPTER 28

*I*n the aftermath of the mill fire, Charlie's lineage was forgotten. Nicholas rarely saw Rebecca, so busy was she helping her father to keep the mill running and fend off creditors.

Three men died in the inferno - all Haitian - their bodies charred beyond recognition. Their identities were known to the foremen on duty when the fire broke out. Insurance investigators spent weeks on site determining the cause of the blaze and estimating damages.

Inside the mill, the smell of burnt sugar mingled with the odor of burned flesh created a nauseating sickly-sweet smell similar to alcohol. The ground around the mill became the repository for the stomach contents of those investigators foolish enough to eat breakfast or lunch before stepping inside.

~

Followers of Vodou believe that death is not the end but the beginning of 16 new lives. They believe that the deceased will be reborn eight times as a male and eight times as a female.

In the Vodou faith, when someone dies, their soul lingers on earth for a week after his or her physical death. During this time, a priest or priestess performs various rituals to release the soul from the body. Once released, the soul remains in "dark water" for the next year.

Vodou followers believe that, if this ritual is not performed, the soul of the deceased will be left to roam the earth as a bad omen. Those souls that are released are believed to reside in a clay jar called a govi. From that jar, they offer guidance to their family members.

Honoring the dead is very important to the Haitian people, who are known for celebrating their culture by worshiping those who lived before them. Rich or poor, Haitians believe their future depends on paying homage to their ancestors.

It is a Haitian custom to entrust the oldest family member with planning the funeral. Since most of the field workers did not have family nearby, that responsibility fell to Edeline. She held a vigil, which all of the workers attended. They banged their drums and chanted and danced around a bonfire that had been set in the middle of the village. With no bodies to bury, five empty coffins were placed on the ground in memory of those who had perished at the mill.

The priestess had personally invited Nicholas, Lamont and Sadie to attend the ceremony. Rebecca came along at Nicholas' request. Nicholas inquired why there were two extra coffins. The answer he received from the priestess created deeper misgivings about the treatment the men and women employed by Otto Bryant received.

"Three men perished in the flames, but five men did not come home."

The priestess refused to expand on her answer. Instead, she challenged Nicholas to "… find the truth for yourself. Life and death in Bryant Village are not what you imagine them to be."

As she spoke, the priestess directed Nicholas to look at a nearby tree from which was hanging a cloth doll dressed in a sugar sack. The normally white sack had been dyed red, but the Bryant label was clearly visible in the center. Nicholas had been told not to wear red to the ceremony as red was the color attributed to an assassin. He did not know then but would soon learn that hanging the doll upside down was a message that the workers intended to make the assassin pay for his crimes. He wondered if Rebecca knew the significance of the display.

At the end of the wake, the five coffins were hoisted on the shoulders of 20 strong men and carried around and around the village. Each time a coffin passed by the doll hanging in the tree, the men would slow their pace, and the man closest to the doll would stick a pin in it. The message was clear. Pain for pain. Death for death.

CHAPTER 29

*O*tto Bryant was anxious for the insurance investigators to be gone. He equally hated having members of the fire departments arson squad on premises. These men were a distraction for the workers, who were constantly having to stop working to answer questions. Whatever the outcome of the two inquiries, the monetary cost to Bryant Sugar would be crippling.

Trying to hedge his bets, Otto ordered Rebecca to remove all records for the men victimized by the fire… the three who died and the two who had mysteriously disappeared. When Rebecca questioned the missing men, Otto told her they had probably run away. The explanation sounded hollow but, being a loyal daughter who lived off daddy's money, Rebecca did as she was told.

The undercurrent of unrest that had existed among the field and mill workers prior to the fire grew stronger every day. The men and women began to loudly voice their discontent with their working conditions. They no longer hesitated to express their distrust for the men Otto had put in supervisory positions and, more importantly, they openly railed against Otto and the harsh way he treated them. The word *rayi,* which meant hate in Creole, was spoken so often, it began to sound like the ending to a prayer.

During the evening devotionals, Edeline prayed to the gods, asking for strength and guidance. She knew that everything had an expiration date... even fear.

For the workers, the fear of fighting back against Otto was being replaced by the fear of what would happen if they did not stand up for themselves. Under Edeline's guidance, they began to believe that if enough people fought back at the same time, evil could be undone and worlds could be overthrown, especially insulated worlds like the one Otto Bryant controlled in Pahokee.

Nicholas did not return to the Village in the first few weeks following the fire. He knew that Haitians mourned for an extended period after the death of a loved one and, with so many deaths to mourn, he wanted to give the villagers the respect they deserved. He was anxious to speak again with Eloise and Charlie, but time was on his side... or so he thought.

Haitians are filled with a revolutionary spirit, born of a time when they were treated as less than human by mercenaries who took them against their will and shipped them across the Atlantic to do back-breaking labor on white-owned plantations.

With the rumblings of unrest among the mill and field workers growing to a deafening pitch, tension was thick and nerves were strained. Evenings in the Village were spent banging drums, dancing, drinking rum and ceremoniously slaughtering pigs to beckon and feed the spirits. The meat of the pig was then cooked and eaten by the villagers.

Nicholas and Lamont were getting nervous. They talked often about the possibility of another protest against the Bryant family. Both men believed that Otto was in danger, but neither of them thought that he feared retribution. They did not think that Otto feared anyone or anything. They were still too naive to know that, when it came to punishment, Otto was the one holding the whip.

~

Needing desperately to put his doubts about Rebecca to rest, Nicholas decided to visit Eloise Weatherby one evening after she had completed her duties at the Bryant house. While Eloise did not actually live in Bryant Village, her house was so close to the boundary line as to be a toe length away. She considered herself one of them, even though by virtue of her ethnicity, she was someone much different.

The sky was dark when Nicholas arrived. He could see a light in the living room window, and a shadow liking on the front porch. Someone was sitting quietly on the top step, watching him. Nicholas' breathing became shallow. He was instantly on guard.

Suddenly, the figure stood up. A halo of gold glimmered in the moonlight, and Charlie smiled in welcome. He was holding a knife deftly in one hand and a block of wood in the other.

"Hello, Mr. Grant. Did you come to talk to me?" The words were stilted but clear.

"Yes, Charlie. Is that a knife you are holding?"

"I'm making a sailboat, like yours. My grandfather taught me to whittle. Can you whittle?"

"No, I cannot, but I would like to learn. Will you teach me?"

Eloise watched from the window as the no-longer-wary boy and the no-longer-hesitant man became friends. Mostly, Nicholas let Charlie talk and, having no guile, Charlie's words were filled with the innocence of youth and the painful truths of one who had learned about life the hard way. As stories slowly poured from his lips, his hands moved with speed and dexterity across the wood, revealing the treasure hidden within.

CHAPTER 30

"*L*illian, are you saying that Rebecca was Charlie's mother?"

Helen already knew the truth of Charlie's parentage. Sam Weatherby had provided the details the evening he had injected himself into her quiet dinner. Helen did not know why, but she felt it was best not to let Lillian know of the meeting or that she was already aware of the details of her father's mysterious past.

"Yes. And Sam Weatherby, Eloise's son, was his father. When Rebecca was 17 years old, she ran away from home to escape Otto's despotic ways. She met Sam, became pregnant, and Charlie was the result. Rebecca wanted nothing to do with motherhood. Understandable at such a young age.

She gave Charlie to Sam, who was incapable of caring for a baby, and she left. He gave Charlie to his parents to raise. Prison followed... petty crimes but enough to keep him behind bars for a few years. When Eloise's husband died, she was no longer able to keep Charlie. She tried to return him to Rebecca, but Rebecca refused to take him.

Fearing a scandal, Otto, who was furious with Rebecca for withholding such damaging information from him, gave Eloise a job as cook and housekeeper. He paid her well. He gave her a house outside the Village. His largess, and I use that word sarcastically, would continue on the condition that she never tell anyone that Rebecca was Charlie's mother."

"Where was Rebecca when Eloise brought Charlie here?" This was a detail that Sam had failed to provide.

"Rebellion loses its appeal when you do not have money or a man to sustain a luxurious lifestyle. Shortly after leaving Sam and Charlie, Rebecca returned home. She begged her father's forgiveness but remained silent about her wild child ways. Otto forgave her. She went to college and earned a degree. Then, she came back home to work at the mill.

It wasn't until Eloise showed up on their doorstep two years later that the truth became known. Otto had harbored big dreams for his daughter. He saw her married to a prominent man... someone who could further his position as a powerhouse in the sugar industry. Charlie threatened to ruin everything. Otto could not let that happen."

"So, Eloise became an indentured servant in exchange for money and a home for herself and Charlie?"

"On the contrary. Eloise became the thorn in Otto's side. He kept her close to keep her quiet. She was willing to work for the family because she knew that seeing her every day reminded Otto of what he had to lose if he dared to harm Charlie."

"Would Otto have hurt a child to keep his mother's identity a secret?"

"Otto would have done anything to keep the Bryant family's real identity a secret."

When Eloise first arrived in the Village, the workers showed disdain for her presence. They considered her a spy for Otto, someone who would insinuate herself into their lives and cause them trouble. It did not take long for them to realize that the opposite was true. Charlie was the conduit who brought them together. When Edeline met Charlie, she recognized herself in his caregiver. Like Eloise, she was a loving grandmother to an autistic grandson.

The prevalence of autistic behavior in the children of Haiti had been ignored by medical experts. Providing psychological support for the very young was unexplored territory. To the parents and grandparents of these children, the fact that the littlest among them were *different* was a cause for growing concern.

Following the earthquake at Anse-a-Veau in Grand'Anse in 1952, an eruption which killed six and left thousands homeless, a large percentage of pregnant women gave birth to children — mostly, boys — who suffered with emotional problems. The fact that these babies were still in utero when the earthquake happened made their condition incomprehensible to their families. In the womb, they should have been safe from harm.

Edeline, her husband, their pregnant daughter and her husband survived the quake, but her daughter began showing signs of psychopathological distress as a result of the trauma. Childbirth was difficult, causing more mental and emotional stress. By the time the baby was three, he was showing signs of hyperactivity, impulsivity and aggression. Edeline's daughter never fully recovered her pre-earthquake mental and physical health. It fell to Edeline to raise her grandson.

In the eyes of the law, Charlie did not exist. He had been born at home, with Eloise serving as midwife. He was never examined by a doctor and there was no birth certificate attesting to the day he came into the world. He was a non-entity, but he was not alone.

The men and women of Bryant Village, following Edeline's lead, took Charlie in as one of their own. He had many mothers and fathers looking out for him. They played with him and taught him their customs. He learned to speak patois and, often, surprised them with his ability to translate from creole to English quickly.

Since Charlie did not go to school, he amused himself by fishing and roaming the woods surrounding the cane fields. Many hours were spent inside the mill, playing in the hidden corners where the foremen would not see him. If not for the fire, his presence there would never have become a reason to fear for his life.

CHAPTER 31

*S*tore-bought toys were an unheard-of extravagance for Charlie. Most everything he had to play with from the time he was an infant was homemade. Beans in a tin can were his rattle. An old rag stuffed with cotton was a doll. His teething ring was a piece of braided leather. Once he was old enough to walk and wander away from Eloise's watchful eyes, his favorite pastimes were fishing and lassoing small animals and trees with his bola. He always released the animals he caught. None were ever harmed.

The bola was a primitive hunting tool used by the Indians of South America and the Gauchos of Argentina. They became popular with children during the 1960s and 1970s when American toy companies became manufacturing them under the name "Clackers." The toy was little more than two large marbles or wooden balls attached to a long string. The idea was to swing the cord until the balls began hitting or "clacking" together. Charlie's version, made for him by the men of the Village, used rope and two round heavy metal weights. When the weights hit together, they would sometimes spark.

During reconstruction of the mill, a length of burned rope with one weight attached was found in the area where the fire was believed to have started. The second weight was found nearby. This also happened to be the area where Charlie most often played. While there was no way to prove that the toy had caused the fire, the arson investigator's report leaned strongly in that direction. Otto's hatred for Charlie reached life-threatening proportions.

With the kitchen so close to the dining room that every conversation could be overheard, Eloise knew that nothing would pacify Otto but that Charlie be gone... permanently. She would need to sneak him out of the Village before Otto made his move. For that, she would need help.

While the Haitians and the Jamaicans who worked the sugar cane fields might not have liked each other, they were joined in one way... they all liked Charlie. No one was willing to see a child die to appease Otto's need for revenge.

Eloise and Edeline, with help from Nicholas, Lamont, Sadie and the workers developed a plan. It would not be enough for Charlie to disappear. Otto must think his orders were followed, and the boy was dead.

Eloise gave Edeline a pair of Charlie's pants, one of his shirts and his sneakers. Edeline gave them to men she trusted. They took them to the alligator pit. There, they covered the sneakers in molasses and tossed one into the pond. The other, they wedged into the mud along the banks, where it would be found.

A fire was lit in the empty metal oil drum kept near the pond. The shirt was torn into pieces and most of the pieces were tossed into the fire with Charlie's pants. The remaining pieces were singed along the edges and thrown into the barrel after the flames went out.

Nicholas and Lamont took Charlie away, not telling anyone where he would be hidden. Nicholas promised Eloise and Edeline that he would be safe, and they believed him because they had no other choice.

Rebecca never questioned the whereabouts of her son. She knew of her father's plans and never voiced objection. Nicholas' heart was broken, but he no longer needed answers to the questions that had troubled him for weeks. Whatever love he had felt for her had been replaced with a burning need to bring Otto to justice. If Rebecca was found guilty of a crime, so be it.

Eloise left the Village shortly thereafter, but her leaving was of her own volition. No one knew where she went.

CHAPTER 32

a breakfast of fresh coffee and donuts, delivered by Lillian, became the standard start to each day. As the women sat on the schooner's weathered deck soaking up the beauty of the lake under clear blue skies, the ugliness that was Otto Bryant became a knife in Helen's heart. She hurt for her father, a little boy she had never met and all the people who had suffered atrocities at the hands of a man determined to change his ancestry from black to white... no matter the cost.

"How can you remain so calm when telling this story. It is horrible. I can hardly breathe listening to you. This is your family you are talking about, Lillian."

"I know how it sounds, Helen, but times were different then. Sadly, times are really not much different now."

"What do you mean?'

"If you are going to write this story, you need to know all the details... all the ugly, distasteful details. I will tell you if you are willing to remain quiet and listen."

∼

Otto was not a stupid man. He knew that Charlie's presence in the mill was enabled by the workers. He was relentless until he learned the names of those who had been on duty the day of the fire. Their punishment was to be the same as Charlie's. They, unfortunately, did not have anyone to help them escape.

Following Otto's orders, the mill workers were brought to the pond, covered with molasses mixed with cement and thrown into the pit. Once the molasses was on the workers' skin, it was impossible for them to lift their arms or kick their legs. They could not scream because their mouths had been sealed shut.

Alligators are basically lazy animals. They prefer small prey, which do not fight back and can be swallowed in one gulp. While they are patient hunters and will stalk their prey through the water for hours, they do not want to work hard for a meal. Prey that fights back, like human beings, is typically abandoned once the thrashing begins.

Pouring molasses over the unfortunate workers served a dual purpose. As a regular part of the alligators' dietary routine, they were accustomed to eating it. The heavy, sticky sweetener also rendered the wearers unable to defend themselves.

"On the night the men were taken, Nicholas went to visit Eloise. Driving through the Village, he saw Otto's pickup in the center of town and felt a premonition that something bad was going to happen. He was in the habit of using Roosevelt's truck when he needed wheels and, feeling a sudden need for secrecy, he parked it out of sight behind Eloise's house.

Nicholas knew what Otto had planned to do to Charlie. He had heard stories of other men who had met their fate at the alligator pit, but he had never actually seen a man killed. Without seeing it happen, it was impossible to believe.

When his visit with Eloise was over, your father decided to walk to the pond. He was quiet; his natural instincts warning him to be careful. What he saw... he screamed in fear and rage. Otto's men gave chase, but Nicholas got away. He ran back to Roo's truck and drove to the marina, intending to pack his bags and get out of town. Your dad knew his life was worth nothing now that he had witnessed Otto's depravity."

"Oh, my God. What happened?"

"Lamont was at the marina waiting for him. One look at your father and he knew something terrible had happened.

Lamont was no fool. He, too, realized Nicholas' life was over if he remained in Pahokee. With a little help from the Chosen brothers, your father was smuggled out onto the lake and out of Okeechobee country."

"I'm going to be sick."

CHAPTER 33

"*D*rink this." Lillian pulled a small flask from her purse. "It will settle your nerves."

"Settle my nerves? Your family wanted to feed my father to alligators!"

"Drink. There is still a lot you do not know."

~

"Nicholas! What happened?" Lamont's voice was frantic with worry.

A duffel bag over his shoulder, Nicholas appeared on deck. "I'm leaving, Lamont. I cannot stay here."

"Tell me what happened?"

~

Shaking from head to toe, Nicholas Grant told Officer Lamont Minor what he had seen. The deputy, shocked to his bones, sat down and covered his face with his hands.

"I knew... I knew, but I did not want to know. I have to do something. I have to investigate, but, Christ... Otto is so powerful. No one will believe me, and I could find myself sweetened and fed to the gators."

"You have to stop him, Lamont. And, I have to get out of here. If Rebecca asks for me, make up a story. I don't care what you tell her. I am never coming back."

"You will never get out of town without help. Trust me."

Noth Chosen, healed from his hip surgery, was back to his old self. He loved night fishing and, as luck with have it, his boat could be seen off in the distance. Lamont grabbed a flare gun from the emergency box on deck and shot it into the air. Nothing! Noth's boat showed no sign of changing direction.

"Roosevelt and Noth. Father liked them a lot." Helen's voice was quivering.

Lamont fired a second flare and, again, Noth seemed unaware of the call for help. Precious minutes passed. Lamont and Nicholas were growing desperate when, suddenly, Noth's boat turned toward shore and picked up speed.

"Roosevelt happened to be with Noth that night. The brothers did not hesitate to bring your father aboard. With barely a glance over his shoulder, your father turned his back on what he thought was his destiny. The chapter of his life that began when his boat got caught under the bridge was over."

"The boat... That's it! I need to know more about this boat."

"What? Why? This boat has rarely been out on the water in decades."

"When I was a child, my father had another boat. We spent many, many happy hours on it. That is what I have been dreaming about. I saw the boat's name - *Qwerty* - written on the side. When I was young, I did not know what the word meant, and my father refused to tell me. He said it was a 'mystery.'"

"Where are you going?"

"It is your turn to follow me."

Helen leapt like a gazelle off the boat and landed with unexpected grace on shore. She immediately turned to look at the stern, where the boat's name was painted - NAUTICAL GYPSY.

"That cannot be right. The name... It doesn't make sense."

Helen stepped back and stared at the spot where the boat's name had been immortalized using vinyl letters. The letters were showing signs of wear and tear from age and the weather. They were peeling away in places, revealing something written underneath.

Frantically, Helen began to scrape at the letters with her fingernails. Another name was revealed. TYPEWRITER.

Helen shrieked. "This makes everything so clear. *Qwerty* is the name given to the center row on a typewriter keyboard. My father named his new boat in memory of this boat."

"Why would he do that?"

"I guess he never forgot his life here or the people who were such a big part of that life."

"When your father arrived, the name of the boat was printed on a board that hung over the stern. Rebecca painted it on the boat for him. Noth covered up the name with the vinyl letters after your father left so that Otto would think he had sailed away."

"What happened to Otto and Rebecca after my father left? And where was Charlie?"

"To paraphrase Paul Harvey, the famous radio broadcaster back in the day... 'And now you will know the rest of the story.'" Lillian's smile was sad. She fought to hold back her tears, not wanting Helen to see the pain she was feeling.

"When Nicholas had to run for his life, Rebecca realized how much she loved him and what she had sacrificed to live as her father wanted her to be. She asked Lamont to contact the State Attorney General. She testified against her father and was given immunity as part of a plea deal."

"What! She could have gone to prison for aiding and abetting." Helen's eyes were the size of saucers. Surprised did not even begin to explain the look on her face.

"Rebecca was never directly involved in the killings. She knew of them but was unable to stop them due to Otto's emotional manipulation. The prosecutor saw her as a victim of her father's cruelty, just as were the workers.

Rebecca's lawyers argued successfully that she was her father's hostage, and, therefore, a victim of trauma bonding. Otto's constant threats to wreak violence upon her and Charlie made her compliant with his demands."

Otto was arrested, tried and found guilty of crimes against humanity, including murder. Without a body, murder cases are difficult to prove, but here is where the alligators played a vital role in Otto's conviction.

Hunters captured four of the largest reptiles in the pond and subdued them while a veterinarian took samples of residue from between their teeth. Human skin cells were found as well as small pieces of tissue and muscle. Remnants of undigested human bones were found in the skat that was plentiful around the pond.

Many of the mill and field workers testified against him. The most convincing of those witnesses was Edeline. She spoke eloquently of the fear her people faced every day while working for Otto. She talked about all the men who had disappeared from the Village without a word of good-bye. She knew them all by name, and she knew the dates of their disappearances.

The men who carried out Otto's orders were also found guilty of murder but to a lesser degree because they were terrified for their own lives. They each were sentenced to 25 years with the possibility of parole after serving 10 years.

Eloise returned and testified to the conversations she had heard while preparing meals. She told of how she and Edeline had saved Charlie's life with the help of Nicholas and Lamont. And, while she did not have many flattering words to say about Rebecca, she did say that she always believed Rebecca cared for her son but was afraid to show it.

The trial lasted two weeks. When the verdict was announced, it was anti-climactic. Otto had been tried in the court of public opinion long before he saw the inside of a courtroom.

The fact that no bodies were found played into the sentencing guidelines, and because Otto did not do the actual killing, he was spared the death sentence. That does not mean that he got away with murder.

Humiliation was a big part of Otto's sentence. After all the years of hiding his Jamaican ancestry, he was housed in the black section of the prison. The inmates knew what he had done. They knew how he had treated his own people.

One week into his life without parole sentence, Otto's lifeless body was found on the floor of the shower. He had been beaten mercilessly.

Otto sustained a basilar skull fracture, which resulted in bruises behind his ears and around his eyes. Most of his body was covered with contusions. His nose was broken and the cartilage at the tip of the nose was damaged from being squeezed shut with excessive force. The medical examiner listed burking, a form of suffocation, on the death certificate.

Forty-eight sugar cubes had been shoved down his throat... one for each man presumed to have met his end in the alligator pit. Otto's body was covered with urine and feces."

"That's horrible."

"Yes. Even being as evil as he was, the punishment was almost as unthinkable as his crimes."

"What became of the mill and the workers?"

"Rebecca paid the field and the mill workers all what was owed and gave them bonuses before arranging for them to return to their homelands.

In his will, Otto left the business jointly to Sandra and Rebecca. Sandra divorced Otto shortly after his arrest, but she and Rebecca remained close. Sandra was never a suspect in the case. She was oblivious to all the drama, wrapped up only in her own wants and needs.

When the trial was over, they sold the mill and the fields to the American Sugar Conglomerate. Sandra moved away. Rebecca set out in search of herself. She was gone for many years."

"Where did she go?"

"The shame of being a Bryant and the shame of what she had done to Charlie was more than Rebecca could bear. She left Pahokee, only this time she was not running away so much as running toward. She went to Jamaica and lived among her ancestors. She learned about the strength of the Maroons and how they were willing to die for freedom. She found out who she was, not who her father wanted her to be.

"I keep asking but I never get an answer. What happened to Charlie after my father and Lamont rescued him?"

CHAPTER 35

"*D*o you remember me telling you that Lamont loved Sadie, but she never seemed to be interested in him? Well, she was crazy about him, but she thought his interest in her was just friendship. They went around and around until one day shortly after Charlie's rescue, Lamont got down on his knees in Doc Dozier's office and said, 'Sadie Mae Chosen, you are my chosen one. I love you. Please say you choose me to be your husband.' Corny, right?"

"Sort of... but sweet. Did they get married?"

"They did and Charlie lived with them until he was an adult. They loved him and he loved them. Roosevelt and Noth... they are both dead now... became his surrogate uncles. Charlie spent many happy hours on Noth's boat and in Roo's automobile shop learning how to be independent. He was a whiz with numbers and handled the book-keeping for them."

Eloise was able to retire on the money that Rebecca paid her. She lived near Charlie and spent the last years of her life watching him become the man he is today. It was the perfect ending to an otherwise horrible story."

"And Sam, too. He finally became a father to Charlie."

"How do you know that?"

"Ah, that truly is a story for another day. Tell me... did Rebecca ever see my father again?"

"No, but he did write to her from time to time. Just notes to make sure she was okay. He never shared any personal details of his life. He loved your mother and you so much. Rebecca knew there was no chance of rekindling their romance. Any feelings your father had for her were gone."

"I almost feel sorry for her."

"She never stopped loving him. She missed him, so she kept in touch with Carl Newsome, the man with the fast car. He kept her abreast of your father's life... his marriage, your birth and your mother's passing. She followed your writing career and read all your books."

"Then, she knew the stories were her stories... the ones she and my father wanted to write."

"Yes. It made her proud that you were successful."

"That is nice to hear."

"She attended your father's funeral."

"She did? Oh, I wish I had met her."

"Maybe, you will one day."

A week passed, during which time Helen prepared to return to Boston. Her divorce had been finalized, lawyers for both parties having handled the settlement details. She had no plans to ever see or speak to her now ex-husband again.

Helen knew she would need to find a place to live. The condo had been sold as part of the divorce and the profits split equally. She was thinking of New York. Manhattan seemed like the ideal place to write her novel.

Helen had always lived for culture -- the theater, the opera, libraries and bookstores straining under the weight of greater and lesser minds. She envisioned her evenings being spent at Lincoln Center or on Broadway. Saturdays at the Metropolitan Museum of Art and MOMA would inspire her, while leisurely dinners with people of opposing opinions would influence her writing. None of these places or people could replace her father, but they would fill some of the holes in her heart.

During her last few days in Pahokee, she prepared an outline for the book she would write about her adventures in what she jokingly called Sugar Town.

Her agent was thrilled with Helen's synopsis and anxious for her to get started on the manuscript.

She also made arrangements for Typewriter to be given to a nearby charity. All the repairs would be paid for through a bank account she set up in the charity's name. They would sell the boat and put the proceeds to good use.

On her final morning, Helen awoke to the sound of voices approaching the sailboat. She dressed quickly and went topside.

A woman who looked like Lillian but was not dressed like Lillian was standing on the dock, a man of about 55 at her side. The woman wore a conservative suit with tasteful jewelry, low-heeled pumps and had her long hair styled in a fashionable French twist. The man was tall and lanky. His once corn-colored curly hair now mostly gray and sparse on his head. His smile was wide; his teeth shining like pearls in the morning sun.

"Hello, Helen."

"Hello, Rebecca... or should I say Lillian."

"How long have you known?"

"Always. You see while you were communicating with Carl Newsome, he was communicating with me. Of course, not until I was old enough to understand who you were."

"Why did you pretend not to know who I was?"

"It wasn't my place to reveal your identity. I knew you would tell me when the time was right. If I may ask, why did you change your name and appearance?"

"Almost no one living here today knows who I am, but they all know the Bryant Mill stories. For Charlie's sake, I did not want them to make the connection to me as his mother.

He is a businessman now. When I sold the mill to American Sugar Conglomerate, the deal was contingent on Charlie holding a 50% ownership in the molasses factory. He will be financially secure for the rest of his life.

I think it's time you met my mystery man."

With pride in her voice, Rebecca made the introductions. "Helen, this is my son, Charlie."

"Hello, Helen. My mother said you are Nicholas' daughter. He was my friend. I brought you a present."

Charlie handed Helen a bottle filled with a dark brown liquid. On the label were the words:

Charlie's Sweet Molasses Syrup
A good source of calcium, potassium and iron

~~~~

A product of American Sugar Conglomerate

CHAPTER 36

*O*n the same day that Helen Grant's novel *Charlie's Molasses* made the New York Times best seller list, researchers from the South Florida Ecosystem Restoration Task Force discovered human remains on the property formerly owned by Bryant Sugar. The front-page story drove sales of Helen's book to epic heights and made her name dinner table conversation in homes around the globe.

Anonymity, the one thing that Rebecca and Charlie craved the most, was fading fast as Helen's book became the top news story at every media outlet.

Reporters swarmed Pahokee, hoping to interview Rebecca, who was nowhere to be found. Her son, Charlie, was also missing.

Sales of Charlie's Sweet Molasses Syrup went through the roof. It seemed like everyone wanted to taste the product that enticed alligators to eat their human prey.

Rebecca and Charlie lived together in upstate New York in a house bought for them by Helen. Since the stories in Helen's original books were based on those Nicholas and Rebecca had planned to publish, she felt it was only right to share her success with them.

Sadie and Lamont also moved to New York. They bought a house near the one Helen had purchased so they could be close to Charlie.

Although Rebecca was Charlie's birth mother, and she had rebuilt a loving and trusting relationship with him, Sadie and Lamont were the parents of his heart. The thought of leaving them was distressing for him.

Sadie and Lamont did not mind moving. Their son and daughter, whom Charlie considered siblings, lived in Lake Park, an hour's drive from Pahokee. The son had followed in his father's footsteps and become a law enforcement officer with the Palm Beach County Sheriff's Office. The daughter was an emergency room nurse at Good Samaritan Hospital in West Palm Beach. They spent their vacations with their parents in New York State.

A year after *Charlie's Molasses* became the number one selling book in the world, Rebecca Bryant died. She was 71 years old. Her son was at her side, as were Helen, Sadie and Lamont.

With what little strength was left in her, Rebecca whispered to Helen, "Your father wanted to write the great American novel. Put his name on the cover of your books as your co-author. He was, is and always will be your muse. Take care of Charlie."

Not many people attended Rebecca's funeral, which was held at the marina in Pahokee. Very few residents who had known her during her father's reign of terror were still alive or living in the area. Those who did attend were probably surprised by the requests she had made in her will.

Only bright colors and island patterns were to be worn to the wake. No black was allowed. The music was a mix of rhythm and blues, jazz, and calypso. Bob Marley, Lee "Scratch" Perry, Peter Tosh, Toots and the Maytals... all popular Jamaican singers and musicians... played on a continuous loop during the service. If anyone standing near the casket had looked closely at her face, they would have seen Rebecca smile.

On the ninth night after the funeral, a party was held at the marina to celebrate what Rebecca had called her "... new life of repentance and joy." Traditional Jamaican food was served along with more recognizable state-side dishes. Curried goat and goat soup, cooked green bananas, and white rice as well as meats, cheese, vegetables, salads and fruit. There were banana pancakes, coconut toto cakes, gizzada tarts, steamed banana leaves stuffed with sweet potato and cassava, coconut drop cookies and sweet potato pudding for dessert.

While cremation is not an accepted practice among Jamaicans, Rebecca asked that her ashes be interred at the cemetery of the Church of Saint Thomas the Apostle in Kingston. Helen and Charlie flew to the island and saw to it that she was laid to rest as she had requested. A peaceful afterlife was guarantee and well-earned.

EPILOGUE

*R*ebecca's passing brought many changes, not the least of which was a need to move Charlie closer to Helen.

Charlie was teenager when Helen was born. As an only child, she had always wanted a big brother and, now, she had one. Helen and Charlie had grown close... as close as any blood relatives could be.

Upstate New York was too far for her to travel on a daily or weekly basis. With everyone in agreement, she moved Charlie, Sadie and Lamont to Manhattan. She found a renovated loft in Greenwich Village big enough for the three of them, very near to her own apartment.

Moving to Manhattan was life altering for Charlie. He was fully independent, having the ability to travel about the city on his own and explore places he had only read about. Charlie was an avid reader. Helen got him a library card, and he spent hours with his nose buried in books of every genre. He loved biographies and stories, like *Charlie's Molasses*, based on actual events.

It was not until the family moved into the city that Helen realized Charlie had a photographic memory. He could scan the pages of a book with his eyes and remember every word he saw. More importantly, he could interpret the most complicated texts and relate them back in simple and understandable terms. On a hunch, Helen had his I.Q. tested. The result: 168. Charlie was a genius!

Sadie and Lamont had made sure that Charlie had a basic education. He could read, and he could write. His math skills were awe-inspiring and needed no help from a teacher. His speech patterns became relatively normal and constantly improved once he had people to talk to every day.

Charlie had never been enrolled in school because he never had a birth certificate. Rebecca went to court when she returned from her trip to Jamaica and made sure Charlie was legally her son. By that time, he was too old for elementary and high school. Helen corrected that failing.

Arriving at the loft one day, she found Charlie sitting on floor surrounded by all 32 volumes of the latest edition of the Encyclopedia Britannica. When she asked where and when he had gotten them and how many he had read, his answer was simple. "I bought them today. I have read them all."

Through contacts in the publishing industry, Helen arranged for Charlie to take a college entrance exam. He passed with flying colors. At the age of 53, he completed eight years of elementary school, four years of high school and four years of college in three months. He earned a Bachelor of Science degree in the Social Sciences.

His brilliance with numbers was only surpassed of his ability to understand the most complex psychological problems and explain them in terms that everyone from doctor to student to man on the street could comprehend. He became an expert on personalities like Otto Bryant and, in time, lectured around the world. He did not shy away from his past, choosing to use it as a teaching tool.

Helen continued to write but most of her time was spent writing books for and about Charlie. She traveled with him, handling all the necessary arrangements and making sure that no one and nothing interfered with his routine.

Charlie was already wealthy thanks to his inheritance from Rebecca and the income he made from the molasses business. The vast amount of money he was paid for speaking engagements, he donated to health organizations that worked with autistic children, especially those with savant syndrome.

During a trip to England, Helen met Dr. Jeffrey Rose. He was a renowned academic in the field of child and adolescent psychiatry as well as a professor at New York University. They fell in love and, with Charlie serving as best man, they were married in a lakeside ceremony in Central Park. A reception at the boathouse followed. Charlie wore a wide smile on his face all day long.

Sadie and Lamont eventually moved back to Florida to be near their son and daughter. Their ages were catching up with them, and they wanted to spend their last years with their grandchildren, who now totaled six.

Helen and Jeffrey each sold their apartment and moved into the loft with Charlie. They adopted a little girl on the spectrum, who showed signs of savant syndrome. Now, she, too, had a big brother.

Life was good.

ABOUT THE AUTHOR

Donna M. Carbone, a proud Jersey Girl now living in Florida, is an author and playwright. For five years, her unfiltered opinion column appeared in *The Beacon Magazine*. She was a frequent contributor to the *Jupiter Courier Magazine* prior to it ceasing publication.

Donna is the author of the Cat Leigh and Marci Welles crime

novels set in Palm Beach County. *Through Thick and Thin* and *Silk Suit/Stone Heart* use the true account of her daughter's kidnapping and rape in 2007 to focus a spotlight on crimes against women. The third book in the series, *Total Submission,* is currently being written.

She is also the author of *Private Hell,* which focuses on domestic abuse, a semi-autobiographical crime novel. Her first children's book, *Lambie and Me,* is based on conversations with her grandson, Blake. Donna swears there is a 60-year-old man living inside that six-year-old body.

Donna's play - *Shell of a Man* - the true story of one Vietnam veteran's 40-year battle with PTSD, was presented at various theaters around the country, including the Dallas Convention Center and the Burt Reynolds Institute for Film and Theatre. Her one-man show, *Fear Sells,* was presented at the TEDxJupiter conference in 2013.

Donna is an outspoken advocate for victims of violent crimes and better healthcare for our veterans. She is a huge supporter of literacy and promotes indie authors in Palm Beach and Martin Counties through her *A Novel Approach to Literacy* author meet and greet events.

In 2018, she published *Bread and Bullets: the Rosario Liotta Story.* Liotta, a recently released convicted criminal, hired Donna to write the true account of what happened to put him in prison for 12 years — a total miscarriage of justice.

"Meeting Rosario and learning more about our criminal justice system has been both a personal and professional blessing. *Bread and Bullets* is just the first of many books we hope to author together. Writing *Charlie's Molasses,* based on an idea by Mark Risher, has also been an opportunity to learn more about people, places and the injustices perpetrated upon the innocent."

You can learn more about Donna on her website: writeforyoullc.com

amazon.com/author/donnamcarbone

THE MAN BEHIND THE STORY

Mark Risher is the first great grandson of Grover and Sylvia Hill, a pioneering couple of Hendry County, Florida. Grover and Sylvia, who were originally from Nebraska, moved to Florida in the early 1900s. They homesteaded on the outskirts of the city of LaBelle, situated on the south side of the Caloosahatchee River. They are considered a founding family in the area.

Fast forward through the years. Mark's father and mother lived in the rural community of Fort Denaud. The region stretched for miles along the south banks of the Caloosahatchee River. While an array of farmers and ranchers called the area home, citrus growers were the primary residents. The area, which became known for growing superb oranges and grapefruits, hosted groves ranging in size from a half acre to hundreds of acres.

From his earliest years, Mark has had an innate love of the land. When just a boy, he helped his father plant the family's first orange grove. A common practice in those days was to irrigate the trees with water from the river. Mark helped to run pipes which carried the liquid sustenance needed to keep the groves alive. Every orange plucked from the trees was a source of pride for him.

Nestled among the fields of citrus trees were small plots of sugar cane. At the time, sugar was not yet the thriving industry it is today, and manpower was in short supply. Every spring during the 1960s and 1970s, Mark and his father helped a nearby neighbor in the making of cane syrup and molasses. A quick learner, it did not take long before Mark became an expert on that aspect of agricultural development.

When Mark was old enough to drive, he took ownership of an old Ford tractor and began a grove service, utilizing his years of expertise working beside his dad. His business grew, and he became quite successful until citrus canker and citrus greening killed most of the trees, putting him out of business.

With his extensive background and knowledge of farming, Mark switched gears and became a respected figure in the tomato industry. He started out as a grower and packer. Eventually, growing tomatoes evolved into the marketing and shipping of various items of produce, which he continues to do today.

The idea for Charlie's Molasses is the result of decades immersed in all aspects of agriculture industry in Florida. Much of what you read in this book is the result of Mark's close and continuous relationships with farmers, ranchers and growers. By listening to the stories passed down from generation to generation, he and Donna were able to join fact and fiction into a story that will both educate and entertain.

ALSO BY DONNA M. CARBONE

The following books are available on amazon.com:

Through Thick and Thin - the first Cat Leigh and Marci Welles crime novel

Silk Suit/Stone Heart - the second Cat Leigh and Marci Welles crime novel

Private Hell - a semi-autobiographical crime novel

Bread and Bullets: The Rosario Liotta Story - a true crime novel

Lambie and Me - children's book

COMING SOON!

Total Submission - the third Cat Leigh and Marci Welles crime novel